DIVINE DORA

BEWITCHED IN HEAVEN

A BESTSELLING NOVEL IN
THE DEMON DIARIES

CLAIRE CHILTON

First published in Great Britain by Ragz Books 2015

This edition published by Ragz Books 2017

Published in Great Britain by Ragz Books

ISBN-10: 1908822538
ISBN-13: 978-1908822536

Bibliography

Adams, Douglas. (2017).
The Hitchhiker's Guide to the Galaxy Omnibus:
The Complete Trilogy in Five Parts.
London, Pan Books.

MORE BOOKS

THE DEMON DIARIES
A Hint of Magic
Bewitched by Magic

Demonic Dora
Bewitched in Hell

Deceased Dora
Bewitched in Death

Divine Dora
Bewitched in Heaven

A Hint of Hell
Bewitched by Christmas

DEDICATIONS

This book is dedicated to Jonathan Eldred for his help with this series and the characters in it, especially Lucian.

ACKNOWLEDGEMENTS

Thank you to Scarlett Olguin for being one of the first of many amazing readers and supporters of The Demon Diaries.

A special thanks to Michelle Hoffman for being a truly exceptional beta reader.

And thank you to all the wonderful fans and readers for joining me on this series. Without you, the stories wouldn't exist.

I hope they made you smile.

"The knack of flying is learning how to throw
yourself at the ground and miss."
— *The Hitchhiker's Guide to the Galaxy Omnibus*
Douglas Adams (2017) p293.

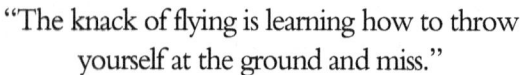

CAMP ANGEL

D ora Carridine threw herself onto the ground with a yelp when she saw a blast of angel fire shooting in her direction. Her pulse raced at the sight of the white flames blazing through the dark sky towards her.

Turning and falling at the same time, she widened her eyes at the sight of the muddy bog below her before she landed face first in a ditch with a loud splat as the holy fire exploded behind her, causing the ground to shake from the eruption.

The cold earth squelched through her fingers as she clawed into it, trying to push herself up. Her exhausted muscles trembled when she rolled over with a groan, swiping the mud off her face and staring down at it in horror as little pieces of glitter sparkled in it.

Fucking glitter mud!

She shook her head. Only in Camp Angel would the dirt be sparkly.

"Get off your ass, recruit!" A deep voice bellowed

beside her.

She turned her head to see Sergeant Fluffers towering over her, his golden chest plate reflecting light around him like some kind of god as his golden hair fluttered in the breeze behind him.

"Piss off, Fluffy," she muttered under her breath at her unrelenting drill sergeant.

"What did you say?" He bellowed as he clenched his hands into giant fists. The blood rushed to his face, reddening it as a vein throbbed in his forehead.

She sighed, biting back the urge to repeat herself. She knew that if she rebelled again, the punishment would be ridiculous—like that time they'd made her do speed ballet for twenty-four hours. "I said *this stuff is sloppy.*" She pointed to the mud.

"Well, that's a very acute observation. Now, GET YOUR ASS UP AND KEEP GOING!" Fluffers went from sane to psycho in a split-second.

She scowled at him, her muscles still aching from the assault course she'd had to fight her way through so far.

He narrowed his blue eyes as a ball of white angel fire ignited in his left hand. "Perhaps you need motivation." He raised his hand.

Widening her eyes, she realized that he was serious. Scrambling to her feet, she ignored her aches and pains as she waded through the bog as quickly as she could, nearly losing her boots to the suction of the thick slop in the process.

After she'd crawled out of the bog, she heard a whoosh of angel fire behind her and threw herself sideways into a copse of trees to avoid being hit by Fluffers' fireball.

"You fucking psycho!" she cried, unable to contain her feelings any longer.

"You'll never get your wings with that attitude, Recruit." She heard him shout back.

Hurrying into the forest, she darted through the trees. "I don't want my fucking wings. I'm not supposed to be here!" she cried as she dodged sharp branches and tried to get as deep into the forest as she could.

She hitched her breath when she heard the whoosh of angel wings overhead. Then she dropped to the ground, hiding under the cover of thick branches while staring up through the gaps between the leaves at the troop of angels who flew by, dropping bombs on innocent recruits.

"Heaven sucks," she muttered, allowing herself to rest for a moment against the trunk of an old tree.

She pulled a strand of her dark hair off her face, narrowing her eyes as mud dripped off it. Peering down at her fatigues, she sighed. The gray camouflage was completely obscured by caked-on, glittering dirt. She closed her eyes, trying to ignore the cold clammy feeling of her clothes against her skin and the shivery feeling from her trembling muscles. She didn't know how long she'd been stuck in Heaven for now, but it seemed like months, maybe even a year.

Not just stuck in Heaven, I'm stuck in angel fucking boot camp!

She sighed. When she'd died and mistakenly been sent to Heaven instead of Hell—which must have been an admin error since she was half demon—she'd thought she'd have found a way back to Earth and her body by now. But they'd mistaken her for a new angel, so she'd been consigned to her own personal hell, Camp Angel, which had turned out to be some kind of sadistic training camp for angels.

Why is this place even in Heaven? What about peace, love and understanding? Since when were angels militarized?

Realizing that the patrol had flown by, she boosted herself up and ran deeper into the woodland. If she could just hide out in here long enough, maybe she could avoid the crazy assault course.

Today was the day she was supposed to prove her worth as an angel. If she passed the tests, she'd get her angel wings, but she didn't want her wings. She wanted to get out of Heaven and go home, preferably as a human.

Hunching her shoulders and adjusting her halo, she ducked under the branches and raced through the trees, scanning the brush for signs of patrols. Right now, she needed to get out of here. But so far, she hadn't found a way out of Camp Angel.

If I skip the tests, maybe they'll kick me out.

Optimistic at the idea of flunking out of angel boot camp, she headed for the perimeter fence. It was the biggest crime to mess with the fence, let alone try to get over it. It would be perfect for pissing off Fluffers enough to kick her out. Failing that, she might actually get over the fence and get out of here on her own.

As she broke through the trees, roughly facing the same direction as the perimeter, she paused. You couldn't miss the glowing golden lattice of the fence that surrounded the camp. It shone like a beacon of crossed wires in the night.

She peered up at the sky to ensure that no patrols of psycho angels were flying by, but the sky was clear. The moon shone brightly along with a sprinkling of stars. There were no clouds for angels to hide behind. The coast was clear.

Breaking her cover of trees, she bolted towards the fence, pumping her arms and legs to cross the muddy ground as fast as possible.

Cold sweat beaded her body, making her gray uniform damp and clingy as she rushed towards her salvation. If she got out of here, she could go home. So what if the other side of the fence was a wasteland full of monsters. It was better than being stuck in here with Sergeant Fluffers and his army of lunatics.

She hitched her breath as she neared the fence. It was the closest she'd ever been to the perimeter. A dangerous humming sound came from the golden threads of energy that crisscrossed around the camp, joining at the golden gates.

Frowning at the fence, she tried to think of a way to get over it. If what she'd been told was true, it would fry any angel who touched it. She hurriedly scanned the glowing lattice, trying to find a way to get through without burning her ass off. Her pulse raced at the sound of blasts in the distance. Other recruit's cries echoed in the night, causing a shiver to shoot down her spine.

I guess the patrols found them.

Galvanized by the need to escape, she reached out to touch the fence. Burning sounded better than having a pair of angel wings welded onto her back.

I'm half demon anyway. Maybe I'll heal.

Wincing, she reached out to touch the golden fence, expecting it to burn. She paused when something tickled her fingers. Widening her eyes, she stared at the fence. Her hand was resting on it, but the angel fire was having no effect at all.

Oh, you're kidding me. All this time I've been fearing an angel blast, and they feel like cuddles!

Rolling her eyes, she gripped the fence and pulled herself up. If this was all the angel armies had for firepower, she was getting the hell out of here right now.

She scaled the fence, losing her footing a few times before she pulled herself up to the top. When she reached the top, she flipped herself over, preparing to drop to the other side while trying to ignore the overwhelming urge to hug someone. The fence seemed to be instilling her with warmth and happiness that she'd never experienced before.

Fluffy bunnies…

She smiled at the idea of being surrounded by warm, fluffy bunnies.

Shaking her head, she scowled.

What the fu—hot chocolate fudge cake…

She paused on the top of the fence, trying to clear her head, but all she could think about were warm and happy things, which were alien to Dora's mind. She tried to throw herself over the fence to escape the camp and the sugary thoughts, but the lattice had woven around her wrists and legs.

She glanced down in horror as she tried to free her limbs from the snaking golden threads that were surrounding her in a cocoon of warmth.

Oh shi—warm cookies and hugs… Motherfu— snuggles and unicorns…

She struggled to get off the fence, but the mind-fuckery from it was filling her with so many warm and happy thoughts that she couldn't stop thinking about them. A small part of her, the part that she mostly ignored, really did want to hug a fluffy bunny.

She slumped into the warm embrace of the fence, curling up into a ball and smiling as she closed her eyes.

Warm blankies and hot cocoa…

"Okay lads, you can turn it off now." The voice filtered into her cocoon. It was harsh, so she chose to ignore it.

The warm humming abruptly ceased before she was thrown out of the cocoon. Opening her eyes in horror as she was tossed onto the cold ground below, she let out a yelp of surprise. Her breath exploded out of her as she landed on the hard soil, her teeth chattering on impact.

After a groan of pain, she peered back at the booted feet of an angel, her eyes traveling up his plated armor until she found herself staring into the angry eyes of Sergeant Fluffers.

She dropped her face back into the muddy earth in defeat, waiting for the inevitable punishment.

There's no hope for me. I was defeated by fucking hugs!

2

HEAVENLY RAINBOWS

Kieron Lascher frowned at the rainbow of light that was glowing in the distance. He pressed back against the shiny silver walls of the sewer, his pulse racing. Being a demon in Heaven was dangerous, but he wasn't going to leave without his Dora-minx. He knew she was here somewhere. He just had to find her and take her home.

Assuming she can go back to Earth…

Since her body had faded from his arms the second he stepped through Heaven's back door, he'd been suffering from panic attacks. Without knowing where she was or where her body had gone to, he was beginning to lose hope of ever finding her.

Clenching his fists, he refused to allow his doubts to stop him. He was going to find her or die trying.

He turned to face Lucian, pointing to the rainbow

of light that was bobbing towards them. "What is it?" He hissed. Lucian was a pain in the ass, but since he was a fallen angel, he was the only guide they had in this alien terrain.

"Ooh pretty," Pooey said as he stared at the lights.

Lucian shook his head at the little brown demon. "It's shit, angel shit. Don't demons fucking know anything?" The dark-haired angel stared at Kieron with disappointed dark eyes. "Didn't your mother teach you anything useful?"

Kieron scowled at him. "She taught me a lot more than my loser father ever did." He stared pointedly at Lucian. Since discovering that the fallen angel was his real father, Kieron was finding it difficult not to punch the guy, if for no other reason than his screwy genetics stunting the growth of his demon horns with goddamn angel genes.

He idly wondered if Lionel had known that he wasn't his son. It would explain a lot about his childhood. In some ways, he almost pitied Lord Lascher. No wonder he'd always been disappointed in him. On some level, he must have known that Kieron wasn't a full demon or his son.

I'm still a demon though. Angel genes or not, I refuse to be a fucking angel.

"Are you fucking with me?" Pooey said. "Angels shit out rainbows? Do they wipe their asses on unicorns too?"

Lucian narrowed his eyes. "If you insult Peggy one more time, you shit-colored fur ball—"

"She likes the name Skanky." Pooey interrupted, referring to Lucian's flea-bitten unicorn, which they'd had to leave behind on Earth.

Kieron thought the creature was better off on Earth and in the safe hands of Mortimus, who had taken great care of her. He wasn't sure if mythical creatures could suffer cruelty, but Lucian's unicorn had stunk until Mortimus had cleaned her up.

"Just because you have a name that basically means excrement, it does not mean that all creatures should suffer the same fate." Lucian poked a finger into Pooey's little chest, which wasn't the best idea because the small demon—who looked a bit like a teddy bear in his current state—latched onto it with his teeth and bit down.

Kieron sighed as he watched Lucian dance around the tunnel with a fluffy, angry demon attached to his finger by its teeth. Frustrated, he brushed his hand through his short blond hair, shaking his head.

They're going to get us caught if they don't shut the fuck up.

"Will you two fucking behave?" He tried to get between them, but Pooey growled at him, clinging on to the angel's finger. Meanwhile, Lucian was dancing up and down, yelping.

Heavenly music echoed down the sewer as bright

11

lights lit up the ground. They all stopped and stared as what could only be described as a rainbow-colored turd floated past them emitting angelic sounds.

Pooey's mouth dropped open in shock, releasing Lucian's finger in the process as he watched the rainbow of colors float by. He inclined his head sideways as he watched it, his expression a mixture of awe and horror. "They sing to you too?"

Lucian closed his eyes as if in silent pain for a moment. "They didn't used to. They must have changed the process since I was last here, fucking idiots!" He slapped his forehead.

"That's kinda creepy." Kieron pointed to the singing turd as it floated by. "Why make it sing?"

Lucian threw his hands into the air. "Like I'd fucking know. Angels, man, they're all fucked in the head."

"But you're one," Pooey said.

"Not anymore," Lucian muttered.

"So your crap doesn't—"

"No, it fucking doesn't!" He glared down at the little demon.

"Aww Fallen Dick, did they leave you out of the shit upgrade? Never mind. You can just eat a box of crayons if you want to see a rainbow. I'll sing for ya." Pooey cleared his throat and then began to growl out a tune that did not sound heavenly at all.

"I'm gonna have to kill him," Lucian muttered

before launching himself at Pooey.

Kieron grabbed the angry angel, holding him back. "That's enough! Stop it. Both of you need to chill the fuck out. We're here to find Dora, and we're not going to do that if we get caught, so stop fucking bickering!"

Pooey held his hands up. "I was only trying to be helpful." He flashed an innocent look.

Kieron narrowed his eyes at him.

"Okay, okay, I'll stop for Dora." The demon lowered his voice. "Sorry, Lameo-Lucy," he muttered under his breath.

Lucian clenched his jaw. Then he stopped struggling to kill the little demon. "So you should be."

Pooey scowled at him.

"And I'm sorry that you have a shitty name," Lucian added.

Kieron rolled his eyes. It wasn't the best apology in the world, but it would have to do. "Okay, good. So we need to get out of here. Which way do we go?" He pointed to the junction ahead, two tunnels leading off in different directions.

Lucian strode into the left one. "This one will take us to the City of Angels." He sighed, which is going to royally suck," he muttered as they headed down the tunnel.

Kieron hurried after him, hoping that Dora would be safely waiting for him in the City of Angels.

Please let her be okay.

"You need to know some stuff before we go up there," Lucian said as they stared up at the shiny golden ladder that led up out of the sewers. "First, *never* tell anyone that you are a demon. Being a demon is bad here. You also don't want to be a sinner, a human, a mammal or different in any way. In fact, the only thing you are allowed to be is an angel. If you're anything else, you'll get blasted to death by angel fire."

He peered at Pooey. "In your case, don't speak. You'll only survive if they think you are an angel's pet, so you can be my shitty, little dog."

Pooey narrowed his eyes and peered at Kieron. "I'm not loving this plan."

"Second." Lucian continued. "You need to act like angelic beings. That means no swearing, no fighting, no killing unless ordered to do so, and no doubt. You need blind faith in the lord, Heaven and being good. If someone tells you to kill a puppy for the lord, you do it."

"I'm not killing a puppy." Kieron shook his head.

"Just distract them by talking about the gigantic rainbow that came out of your ass that morning instead," Pooey advised with a nod.

Lucian covered his eyes with his hands and shook his head. "Oh fuck, we're all gonna die."

"Stop being so doubtful, Angel-fail." Pooey

jumped onto the first rung of the ladder and began climbing up it. He glanced back over his shoulder. "They're fucking angels. How scary can they be?"

GET YOUR WINGS

A cold shiver of fear shot down Dora's spine as she listened to Sergeant Fluffers whistling a jaunty tune. She couldn't see him due to the black hood over her head, but she was certain that whatever he had planned for her would not be good.

Gritting her teeth, she tested the shackles, trying to break out of them. But the cold metal was solidly clamped around her wrists, binding her hands behind her back.

She considered making a blind run for it, but gave up on that idea when a meaty fist pushed down on her shoulders, forcing her to kneel.

Trying to see through the hood was impossible. The dark material was thick and coarse. She was completely engulfed in darkness.

Giving up any attempts to fight the panic bubbling up inside her, she openly struggled with the restraints, trying to break free. The combination of being blinded and bound was too much. She summoned all of her strength, trying to break out of the cuffs, but the metal held. She didn't summon her demon strength. Even she wasn't that crazy. She knew that the second she revealed the demon inside her, she'd be the new target for angels to shoot missiles at.

With a sigh, she lowered her head. The handcuffs were too strong.

There has to be a way out of this fucking nightmare!

The whistling abruptly stopped, causing a vice to tighten around her heart. She hitched her breath. Her breathing sounded so loud in the ominous silence. Her pulse raced, and a cold sweat popped up on her skin.

What are they going to do to me?

For the most part, her worst punishment in Camp Angel so far had been cleaning the latrines with a broken fairy wand. Scraping crusty rainbows off the floor with a sparkling pink stick had been a pretty bizarre experience, but bizarre seemed to be the norm here.

Narrowing her eyes, she refused to give into her fears.

What's the worst they can do? It's not as if they can kill me.

She wasn't sure, but she suspected that once you were in Heaven, you couldn't die again.

The silence began to grate on her nerves.

"What are you planning to do with me?" she asked, her breath warming up the hood.

There was no response.

She turned her head, listening for hints of other people near her.

"Hello, is anyone there?"

The area remained silent.

Frowning, she waited a beat.

Have they fucking left me here?

Once she was certain that she was alone, she rolled onto her back and looped her arms down her legs and past her feet, so her arms were cuffed in front of her rather than behind her back. Then she struggled to stand up.

Once standing, she slowly turned around, trying to hear a hint of a sound. There was a faint whistling of air around her, but nothing else.

"What the fuck is this bullshit?" She reached up and ripped the hood off her head, nearly losing her balance when she peered around.

She widened her eyes as she stared in horror at the amount of nothing beneath her. Surrounded by only blue skies and a few clouds, she swallowed a bubble of panic when she realized that the camp was just a green dot below her. It seemed miles away. Although in reality, it was probably just a few hundred meters.

She breathed a sigh when she managed to regain

her balance. Then she stared down at the tiny cloud beneath her feet.

A fucking cloud, they left me stranded on a fucking cloud!

The cloud was only two feet wide in diameter, a tiny platform that was stopping her from falling to her death. It was so small that she was surprised she hadn't rolled off it when she was freeing her arms from behind her back.

Even though she didn't think she could die here, she wasn't certain. Glancing down at the land below, she fought a bout of dizziness, sinking to her knees to ensure she didn't lose her balance and fall off.

"Assholes!" she shouted, but there was no one here to hear her.

She peered around at the expanse of blue skies. A light breeze blew strands of her dark hair around her face. She brushed them back with her cuffed hands.

I'm screwed.

Rubbing her brow for a moment, she tried to think of how to get back to land without killing herself. The cuffs clinked against the chain, reminding her they were there.

The first thing I need to do is get these things off.

She frowned at the golden shackles. They looked shiny and new. The metal was thick and solid. After studying them for a moment, she realized that they didn't have a lock on them. They looked as if they'd been welded on.

They must have done it with angel fire. Fuck! How do you get unbreakable handcuffs off?

She frowned, trying to decide what to do. Since she'd been here, she'd fought against going into demon form for many reasons, but mostly because she knew it would set off the evil sensors around the camp.

She sighed.

It's the only thing that's going to break angel magic though…

She scanned the skies. There was no one else here to see it, and it seemed to be her only chance.

She summoned her anger, the darkness inside her, trying to bring out the demon within. When the skin on her hands turned red, she narrowed her eyes and tried to break the bonds. The golden handcuffs shimmered as they stretched. With a roar, she broke out of them, the pieces of gold cracking and exploding off before they fell towards the ground far below her.

Lowering her head, she inhaled, expecting her heart to stop or something. When she'd been a half demon on Earth, the demonic part of her had been sucking the life out of her. But here, it seemed to thrive.

She smiled. She felt strong. She felt powerful.

Standing up, she stretched out her wings, glancing back to examine them. They were veiny and red, like the wings of a bat.

I wonder if I can fly?

She peered down at the ground again, this time feeling no fear. If she could fly, she could get past the fence and finally escape Camp Angel. Her eyes widened with realization.

I'm free! I can go home.

She tried to flap her wings, finding it was easy. She just needed to think about it, and her muscles did it for her.

Okay wings, glide me the fuck out of here.

Swallowing back any fears, she leapt off the small cloud and attempted to fly. She yelped when she dropped like a stone out of the sky.

Fuuuuuuuck!

Quickly spreading out her wings and trying to flap them, she felt a bubble of panic growing in the back of her throat. But then she breathed a sigh as they caught the wind, slowing her fall. She glided towards the fence around Camp Angel as she got into the rhythm of flying. It took her a few seconds to master the art of gliding, using her body and the tips of her wings to direct herself past the fence.

It's working. I'm going to make it.

She aimed for outside of the perimeter, her pulse racing as she slowly descended over the camp.

The wind around her picked up, shooting out blasts of cold air.

Frowning, she glanced up to see the cloud she'd been standing on expand and darken to ominous gray.

Little shocks of white lightening were sparking off it.

Oh, come on. What the fuck is that?

The sky rumbled above her and streaks of silver lightning shot out of the cloud, illuminating the sky around her.

She dodged the streaks of light, trying to avoid being fried in mid-air. Her heart pounded as she swooped left and right, trying to avoid being hit. Determined not to end up back in Camp Angel, she pointed down, trying to speed up her journey to the ground.

I just need to get outside of the camp. Come on. Come on.

She stared at the desert, flapping her wings to get there faster.

A loud crack filled the air followed by the roar of a storm. She glanced up to see a streak of lightning heading straight for her. With no time to move out of the way, it hit her squarely in the back with a force that knocked her out of the sky.

Her teeth chattered as she fell to the ground. All she could see was a blinding white light. Her body shuddered as the silver light blasted through her, painfully ripping away at her insides.

Her breath whooshed out as she landed on the hard ground with such a force that her legs collapsed beneath her.

After taking a moment to overcome the shock of

impact, she winced as she pushed herself up, her wings aching on her back, and her eyes still blinded by silver light.

She shook her head, and the silver light moved to the side.

Did I make it?

She brushed her dented halo out of her eyes, relieved to find that she wasn't blind. It was just the glowing halo around her head had slipped over her eyes.

She groaned when she noticed that she was on the wrong side of the fence and realized that she'd landed inside Camp Angel.

Fear pooled in her belly when she saw the Sergeant and the General heading straight towards her in a shiny jeep.

They'll see my demon wings!

Panicking, she looked over her shoulder. Her eyes widened. Her demon wings weren't red any more. They appeared to have sprouted white feathers.

Oh, what the fuck is this?

She flashed her wings, and they spanned out to reveal pure white angel wings.

Jumping to her feet, she stared at the jeep heading towards her.

No, no, no. I can't be an angel.

Narrowing her eyes, she flapped her wings, taking off from the ground and rising up.

Catch me now you fucker—

She didn't finish the thought as a patrol of angels landed on her back, driving her down to the ground and holding her there.

She raised her head as the jeep pulled up, and the general stepped out, his golden boots splashing in the mud as he strode towards her.

He glanced back at Sergeant Fluffers. "You were right about this one. She is determined."

Dora scowled. So what if she was an angel now. At least she could fly her ass out of this place.

The general smiled at her. "Congratulations on graduating and earning your angel wings. Now you're ready to have your mind wiped."

"What?" She struggled to get free of the angel guards. "No, I don't want to. I'm fine, I'm—"

"Full of shit, my dear." The general interrupted. "You've tried to escape this camp several times, and you're just not assimilating to the program." He patted her on the shoulder. "But you are an angel recruit, and we don't give up on our warriors, so you'll be getting some special care during the next phase of your training."

"What, no. I'm good. I'll be good." She nodded, panicking about what they were going to do to her next. She needed to keep her memories. She needed to get home.

"Take her to the compound." The general nodded

to the guards, who flew up into the air with her still in their grasp.

"No, come on. This is bullshit, man. I passed your fucking angel test already," she cried, but the general was already on his way back to the jeep as she was carried away.

THE CITY OF ANGELS

K ieron gaped at his first view of the City of Angels. Gleaming chrome and golden skyscrapers towered so high above him that they seemed to touch the clouds. Angels were bustling through the busy marketplace, some stopping to watch the street performers and others rushing into stores and buildings.

"Lemme look." Pooey pushed between his legs to peer out of the dark alley they were hiding in.

Kieron heard Pooey yelp, and he peered down to see Lucian yank him back into the alley by the scruff of his neck.

He turned around to frown at Lucian. "What are you doing?"

Lucian yelped when Pooey bit his hand, dropping him onto the ground in the process. After rubbing the bite with a scowl, he looked up. "I'm saving dumb-shit bear from getting himself flayed. Although, I do sometimes wonder why I bother."

"God, you fuc—" Lucian slapped his hand over Pooey's mouth before he could finish.

"This is not a fucking tourist trip. You do not take the Lord's name in vain here. Don't even say it unless you want to trigger the alarms." He eyed Pooey. "Also, you best not speak. You'll pass for a harmless bear if you keep your fucking mouth shut."

Pooey stared up at Kieron with big sad eyes before he bit Lucian's hand to make him release him. "This is bullshit, man. Why am I getting singled out here?"

Kieron felt a moment of sadness for the little bear. Lucian was being meaner to him, and a part of him wondered if it was because Lucian was his father, which inspired hopeful emotions that he didn't really want to feel. Luckily, the feeling didn't last for long. It evaporated when Lucian spoke.

"You're getting singled out because I am an angel, and he fucking looks like one." Lucian nodded at Kieron before glaring back at Pooey. "You, on the other hand, look like something that crawled out of fluffy hell," Lucian said to the little bear, who in response bared his sharp teeth at him and growled.

"Why are you so paranoid about this place?" Kieron asked. "They look really friendly." He pointed to the angels who were smiling at each other near the fountain. One of them jumped up and hurried to help an older angel across the street.

Lucian shook his head. "Appearances can be deceiving. The evil that lurks here is far worse than anything you've seen in Hell."

"They all look so sparkly and fluffy. Are you sure you're not just pissed that they kicked you out on your ass?" Pooey muttered as he stared out of the alley.

Lucian did a double take. To be fair, the little demon must have teleported to the entrance of the alley because Kieron had no idea how he'd ninja'd his way out of Lucian's grasp and somehow got to the alleyway entrance so quickly.

"Can we put a fucking leash on him?" Lucian muttered.

"Good luck with trying that bullshit." Pooey glanced over his shoulder.

"My ass wasn't kicked out by the way. I left this place as fast as I fucking could." Lucian glared at Pooey.

"Why?" Kieron asked. He was curious about what had caused Lucian to leave. Sure, he'd heard about Heaven when he lived in Hell. The words 'sanctimonious assholes' were often used in the same sentence as the word 'Heaven'. But from here, the angels looked nice and friendly.

Lucian shook his head. "They're all controlled by assholes. You can't live here. You can only serve."

"But isn't helping others a good thing?" Kieron

asked.

"How did you survive in Hell? Seriously, did you bake cookies for the devil or something?" Lucian stared at him in awe.

Kieron scowled. "I was a really scary demon. There's nothing wrong with being nice once in a while."

"Oh, I bet you were, and being nice is just a means to an end. Even with the best intentions, being nice never ends up nice. You're either doing it because you want something for yourself, or you regret doing it because the recipient is an ungrateful bastard." Lucian's brow knotted into a dark frown. "Don't be so fucking naïve. This place is all about serving yourself."

Kieron folded his arms and scowled at the fail-angel. "So what about that guy?" He pointed to an angel in the center of the square, who was healing a puppy that had chipped its tooth. "What's he getting out of doing something nice?"

"A loyal puppy!" Pooey interrupted. "I like this game. Who's next?"

Kieron narrowed his eyes, scanning the crowds. "Okay, what about her?" He pointed to a woman who was giving clothes out to the poor.

"Free marketing, she's making a name for herself. Those t-shirts have her logo on them." Pooey nodded at the golden t-shirts she was handing out.

Kieron scanned the crowds, trying not to see selfish

motivation behind all the good deeds, but unable to see anything else now he was looking through Lucian's and Pooey's skeptical eyes. "You're wrong. There is good in the universe, the unselfish kind. It's just not here right now."

"Okay, let's take you somewhere else then. Do you want to see the Sinner's Quarter?" Lucian asked.

"Oh yay, I love the Sinners Quarter in Hell." Pooey excitedly clapped his hands.

"I wonder if they have blood cotton candy here too." Kieron smiled. "Yes, let's go there."

"Follow me, and keep your mouths shut." Lucian shook his head as he led them out of the alley.

Kieron's mouth dropped open in shock as he stared at the Sinners Quarter. It was a large square with a maze of streets winding off it. The center of the square was busy with crowds, who were all watching the activities on the center stage.

Over the heads of golden-haloed angels and past the occasional flash of white feathered wings, he saw five angels bound to racks, on display like animals. The angels tied to the racks were beaten and bruised. One had had its wings ripped off, which were lying in a bloody pile at its feet. The white feathers were stained pink with the creature's blood.

Kieron averted his eyes to the next victim, who

appeared to have been flayed recently.

Looking down to avoid seeing the destruction of such magnificent beings, his eyes fell upon Pooey, who was staring wide-eyed at the golden armored angel who was torturing the other angels.

"What the fuck are they doing?" Pooey muttered in a hushed voice. "What the hell is wrong with them?" He pointed to the crowds that were staring in silence at the torture with placid smiles on their faces.

"Welcome to Heaven, where disobeying an order leads to having your entrails ripped out," Lucian said in a dry voice.

Kieron looked up as the armored torturer's hand exploded with a white glow of fire.

"Oh fun, angel fire," Lucian muttered.

Kieron watched the torturer shoot a fireball at the third angel, who exploded into flames, his skin burning off as he screamed in agony.

"What do those uniforms mean?" He pointed to the golden armored angel who was torturing the others.

"Those are the Angel Guard, angel warriors who act as the police and army here. Apparently, they keep order." Lucian rolled his eyes.

"Are they reasonable?" Kieron asked.

Lucian stared at him as if he was insane.

"It's just, one of them is coming over here," Kieron added, nodding at the hulking beast of an angel who was stomping through the crowds towards them.

"Shit. Keep your mouths shut!" Lucian visibly blanched before he straightened his shoulders and turned to face the guard.

"Good morrow, citizen," The angel's muscles tensed beneath his armor as he glared at Lucian.

"Hello there. What can I do for you?" Lucian asked, offering a helpful smile. It was an expression that Kieron had never seen on his face before.

"What manner of creature doest thou harbor?" The guard nodded at Pooey.

"Oh that, that's my dog." Lucian reached down and ruffled Pooey's fur. "He's cute, don't you think?"

Judging by the guard's disgusted expression, he did not think that Pooey was cute.

Kieron's pulse raced as the guard's hand rested on the hilt of his sword.

Shit, he's not buying it. We're screwed.

Pooey stared up at the guard, displaying his biggest, saddest eyes. "Woof," he said.

The guard frowned. Then he shook his head. He turned back to face Lucian. "Good day, citizen." He nodded before turning on his heel and walking away.

"Good work," Lucian muttered. "Now let's get the fuck out of here." He guided them out of the quarter.

"What the fuck was with the Shakespearean-speak?" Pooey mumbled out of the side of his mouth.

"When their minds get wiped, they get uploaded

with the memories of the original angels. I guess he got one from the Golden Age." Lucian glanced back over his shoulder as they hurried down a dark street.

"What, like recycling?" Pooey asked.

"More like brainwashing."

HOLY MIND-FUCK

Dora stared at the solid white door ahead of her as she plucked a shiny topaz pebble out of the bowl on the table beside her bed. She threw the pebble, trying to make it bounce off the door. Unfortunately—because she was becoming increasingly frustrated by being locked into a boring white room—she threw it a bit too hard, and it embedded into the wall instead.

Inclining her head sideways at the wall, she plucked another pebble out of the bowl. She threw a second pebble with all her might, smiling when it too embedded into the wall, creating the beginning of a shiny blue pattern on it.

"At least I can redecorate," she muttered to herself.

She'd been scared when the angels had first brought her here and locked her in the room. She'd been told it was a prison, and in some ways, it was. The door was always locked. She couldn't get out. She'd tried everything she could think of. After being in here for what felt like days, her fear had turned into boredom.

The bed was white. The room was white. Everything was white except for the little blue pebbles. A little machine in the corner delivered fresh bedding and meals at regular intervals, requesting her old bedding and dirty dishes at the same time in a metallic voice.

She had a bed and a bathroom, but nothing else. Without interaction, books, a world to look at, it was the most boring place in the universe.

Occasionally, she started to lose it, freaking out that they were locking her in here forever, but even fear got boring after a while.

Narrowing her eyes, she stared at the door. The never-ending silence was beginning to drive her crazy.

Is that what this is? Are they trying to drive me nuts?

The frustrating part of this was that she didn't know what they wanted. If this was their master plan for making her into a good little angel, then they must be expecting to bore her into submission.

She jumped off the bed and stood up.

Enough of this bullshit. There has to be a way out of here.

She turned around, scanning the room. The walls were smooth. There wasn't a scratch on them. Well, there was now. Her mouth turned up at the corners as she admired her pebbles that had wedged into the perfect surface, leaving cracks and chipped plaster around them.

She exhaled a sigh. She knew that her quest for a way out was a pointless act. She'd already searched the room a hundred times. But with nothing else to do, she decided to try again.

Scanning the room, she studied the locked door, the blank walls and the impenetrable floor, looking for any possible way out but finding none.

Expelling a sigh over her stupid optimism about getting out of here, she froze when her gaze traveled up the wall to the ceiling.

Frowning, she tilted her head as she stared at the white ceiling. She'd studied it many times, never once seeing a flaw or anything in the flat white surface. But from this angle, she could see fine black lines.

Walking over to the wall, she looked up, keeping her eyes locked on the lines as they widened the closer she stepped towards them.

She hitched her breath as she stood directly under them. It was a grate, similar to an air vent. It was well disguised because the bars on it were angled. From her bed, the view of it was camouflaged. While standing beneath it, she could see that it was large enough for her to get through.

It's a way out!

Smiling, she hurried over to the bed. Getting out of here had just become a possibility.

She gripped the end of the single bed, dragging it with her as she backed up towards the grate.

She winced as the bed's legs scraped across the white tiles, emitting a painful screech that echoed through the silent room. Trying to ignore the sound that was grating on her last nerve, she breathed a sigh when she dropped the end of the bed under the grate, and the noise stopped.

Glancing back at the closed door, she listened for sounds of guards. The corridor outside was silent.

Fighting to contain her excitement, she climbed up onto the bed and reached up for the grate, breathing a sigh when she discovered that she could touch the ceiling.

I'm so getting the hell out of here, right now!

She pushed her palms against the grate, smiling when it easily lifted to reveal an air vent. The hole was just big enough for her to fit through.

"Please submit your soiled dishes."

Dora yelped as the metallic voice from the vending machine echoed in the room, causing her to stumble. Losing her balance, she waved her hands in the air behind her for a few seconds before falling back off the bed. Her breath exploded out of her as she landed on her back on the floor.

Groaning, she arched her back, feeling pain in her hips and shoulders. She rolled over onto her side and glared at the machine, which was emanating a flashing red light because it wanted her dirty dishes.

Pushing herself up off the floor, she stood up and rubbed her backside while scowling at the machine.

Bending, she scooped up her plate and hurried over to the machine, dropping the dish into the compartment with narrowed eyes. "Clean that, you fu—"

"Thank you." The machine interrupted. "Please take your bedding and nourishment." A white plastic tray with pre-prepared food shot out of the top slot as a bundle of folded blankets and sheets dropped into the laundry bag that was hooked to the base of the machine.

"Go fuck yourself," Dora muttered. She frowned down at the bedding and food. Why were they giving angels food anyway? Everyone knew that only new recruits needed it because they had yet to break their old human habits.

Her stomach rumbled. In her case, that might not be true. She wasn't sure if she was a demon, an angel or still a human.

She widened her eyes. If she was going to escape, she was going to need these things. She pulled the laundry bag that contained the clean bedding off the machine. Then she snatched up the food tray, dropping that into the bag.

"Thanks for the supplies," she said to the machine as she threw the bag over her shoulder and turned back to face the bed.

"You are welcome," the machine said as she climbed up and pushed open the grate before boosting herself up into the ventilation system.

Scurrying through the vent was slow going because Dora had to keep stopping to adjust her bag. Wincing at the clunks and echoes as she made her way through the dusty tunnel, her heart pounded at the idea of being caught.

Come on, just a little bit further.

Peering down through the grates at the other rooms as she passed them, she knew she was passing over a line of identical cells. Some of the cells were inhabited by silent angels and others were empty.

A shiver shot down her spine every time she passed a cell with a blank-faced angel inside it. They were all the same, wearing white jumpsuits and staring blankly at the walls.

What the fuck's wrong with them?

She breathed a sigh when she peered down through a grate to find a laboratory. It was empty, but at least it wasn't home to an empty-eyed angel.

Slowly exhaling to shake off the feeling of

impending doom, she continued down the tunnel, hoping that it would lead to a way out.

As she neared the next grate, she could hear shouting. Frowning she scurried towards it, peering down through the slats beneath her.

She widened her eyes at the angel below. He was young and handsome, but his face was contorted with anger as he shouted at the angels surrounding him. His arms and white-feathered wings were strapped down to a table, which he struggled against.

"Let me go, you fucking weirdos!" he cried.

"Joseph, you will feel better soon. Calm yourself." One of the other angels told him.

"Fuck you, Dr. Braindead. I know what you're doing. You're going to destroy me!" The bound angel cried. "He'll find out when he returns. He'll stop you."

The older angel, who was wearing a white coat and carrying a clipboard, shook his head. "Poor, Joseph. We're doing God's work. You'll understand soon enough." He expelled a sigh and then nodded to the technician beside him, who pulled a lever.

Blue light shot from one of the machines and into Joseph's chest, causing him to scream in agony before he slumped back onto the gurney.

"You're just working for the corporation. You don't even remember who God was," Joseph muttered as his eyelids fluttered before closing.

"God is the corporation," the man with the

clipboard said.

Dora frowned.

What are they doing to him, and what the hell is that supposed to mean?

After a few minutes of blue light floating into Joseph's chest, the technician pulled the lever, turning it off.

The man with the clipboard hovered over Joseph as he opened his eyes.

"How are you feeling?" The man with the clipboard asked.

Joseph turned to stare blankly at him. "I do not feel, major."

The man with the clipboard smiled. "And where is your God?"

"God is everywhere. He is the corporation." Joseph's voice held no emotion as he spoke, and his blank stare was freaking Dora out.

The man with the clipboard nodded to the technician. "This one's rehabilitated. Who's next on our list?"

Dora widened her eyes.

Oh, fuck no. That is not my destiny.

She hurried down the tunnel, her heart pounding. She felt sorry for Joseph, but like hell her fate was going to be a mind wipe.

Who are the corporation? Since when was God corporate?

Shaking her head, she scurried on her hands and knees towards the grate at the end of the tunnel, focusing on the dim glow of light emitting through its slats.

Please let this be a way out...

She reached the grate and tried to see through it, but it was hard to see through the mesh. Gritting her teeth, she swung around and kicked out at it, knocking out the screws that were holding it in place after a few kicks.

She peered down through the open hole.

The glow was coming from the perimeter fence. On one side was the training ground of Camp Angel. On the other side was the wasteland.

Her pulse raced as she heard alarm bells ringing behind her. Gripping her bag, she jumped down, dropping past the fence and into the wasteland. Then she ran as far away from Camp Angel as she could.

6

THE LIBRARIANS

Kieron held up his candle and scanned the dark room, the candlelight wavering as a breeze wafted through the ornate open doorway behind him. He sucked in his breath at the sight of the main hall in the Library of Enlightenment. What he could make out in the dim lighting was a palatial room with stained glass windows and intricate carvings in the high ceiling. The mosaics on the floor were tinted with gold and pearl, and the long lines of shelves appeared to be hand-carved with marble posts dotted around the perimeter.

He jumped when he heard footsteps behind him, spinning around to see Lucian lounging in the doorway with his arms folded.

"Don't just stand there. Start looking. If Dora's still in this realm, the records about her location will be in here."

"What is this place?" Kieron ran his hand over one of the shelves, brushing his fingers over the spines of the books on it.

"It's just the main library." Lucian shrugged. "The archives are over here." He pointed to the back of the room and then gestured for Kieron to follow him.

"Why did we have to break in through a fucking sewer then?" Pooey asked as he wandered into the room, brushing dirt off his fluffy arms.

"Keep your voice down." Lucian spun around. "The last thing we want to do is wake the fucking librarians up!"

Kieron and Pooey both glanced at each other with questioning expressions.

"Since when are librarians scary?" Kieron asked.

Lucian shook his head. "This isn't Earth. The rules are different here. I'd have thought demons would fucking realize that given the fucked up dimension you come from," Lucian muttered.

"Yeah, but. They're just librarians." Pooey shrugged. "What are they gonna do, take away my library card?"

Lucian pointed up to the ceiling. "Look up, and embrace enlightenment, little ball of fluffiness."

Kieron and Pooey both looked up at the same time. Kieron hitched his breath. He'd missed it when he first scanned the ceiling, but there were angels hanging upside down from it like vampires, their white wings wrapped around them like cocoons, their eyes closed as they slept above, guarding the books beneath them.

"That's just fucking creepy," Pooey whispered. "What happens if they wake up?"

"You'll get to experience having your ass handed to you in a very uncomfortable manner," Lucian replied in a quiet voice. "Let's just find the information we need and get the hell out of here, okay?"

Kieron and Pooey both nodded.

Lucian turned on his heel and hurried down the aisle between a line of reading desks and a line of towering shelves.

Kieron swallowed, trying to shake off the feeling of doom as he followed the fallen angel. He couldn't help but glance up to stare at the silent sentries above him. Their hands were folded across their chests. The only thing that moved was their hair wafting in the breeze as it hung down off their heads, trailing in the air.

He peered at Pooey, who was also staring up at the ceiling as he tiptoed through the room. The little bear shuddered before glancing at him.

"Creepy motherfuckers aren't they?" the little demon whispered.

Kieron nodded. He wasn't sure if it was the fact that they were hanging above him and could wake up at any moment or if it was their statue-like posture and frozen bodies, but they made his skin crawl. His heart was thumping so loudly, he was almost certain that it would explode out of his chest if one of them woke up.

Silently following Lucian to the end of the long hall, Kieron breathed a sigh when they reached a line of ancient filing cabinets that were nestled at the back of the room.

"Short ass, you take the lower drawers, and we'll do the higher ones," Lucian said to Pooey, pointing to the filing cabinets.

Pooey scowled, and he looked as if he was about to say something, but one glance at the creatures hanging above them seemed to silence him. He nodded, pulling open one of the drawers.

"What are we looking for?" Kieron whispered to Lucian.

"If she came here and they thought she was an angelic soul, she'll have been assigned to one of the boot camps. We're looking for her recruitment papers," Lucian whispered.

"What if they thought she was demon?" Kieron asked.

Lucian paused. He shot Kieron a dark look. "You don't want to know."

"Of course I want to know. That's why I asked." He frowned.

Lucian shook his head. "She won't exist anymore."

"What the fuck? That was never a possibility. Why

are you saying that now?" Anger coursed through Kieron's veins. She had to still exist. He couldn't save her if she didn't exist.

"Keep your fucking voice down!" Lucian glanced up at the ceiling.

"I will not. If Dora's been hurt by these fuckers, I want them to wake up, so I can kick the crap out of them." Kieron raised his voice.

"Found it. She's—" Pooey pulled a file out of drawer he had been searching in, but then he froze, staring up with wide eyes as a cold screech filled the air above them

Lucian looked up. "Fuck," he muttered as he drew out the sword at his hip. He glanced at Kieron. "I guess you're going to get your wish."

Bracing himself, Kieron stared up in horror as the room lit up to reveal hundreds of creatures waking up above them. They weren't in the least bit angelic with pinched, long faces and slits for eyes that glowed silver.

The one screeching like an alarm was the first to move, spreading out her wings to reveal sharp golden talons on the tips. Her body was feathered too he realized as she detached from the ceiling and swooped around waking up the other librarians.

She flexed her clawed toes as she circled above them, emitting sharp cries. Her angular face was almost bird-like. He widened his eyes at her sharp, little fangs as she opened her mouth to screech out another cry.

"Oh, that's just fucked up. What are they?" Pooey asked.

"Librarians." Lucian shrugged. "We need to get out of here before the head librarian wakes up."

Kieron was frozen to the spot until Lucian shook his arm.

"Wake the fuck up, idiot son. We need to get the hell out of here."

Mobilized by the realization that more of them were waking up, he nodded and followed Pooey and Lucian as they ran for the doors.

Hearing a whoosh of wings, he ducked down on instinct as one of the creatures swooped down.

The librarian's talons clawed through his shirt, grazing his skin before the harpy-looking creature flew back up into the air.

"Keep moving," Lucian cried as he shot blasts of white light from his hands, knocking the creatures back up above them.

Jumping to his feet, Kieron launched himself towards the doors, joining Lucian and Pooey as the noise in the room reached a crescendo.

He watched hundreds of creatures waking up and swooping around the room as their screeches echoed through it. The only thing keeping them back were the blasts of Lucian's magic.

Pooey covered his ears, shouting over the din.

"They'll wake up the whole fucking city!"

"That's kind of the point," Lucian muttered. "Let's get the fuck out of h—" Lucian froze as a deep growl echoed through the building beneath them. It was so loud that the foundations shook, and the windows shimmered from the echo of it.

"What the hell is that?" Pooey widened his eyes.

Lucian swallowed. "It's the head librarian." After a moment of contemplation, he shoved Kieron and Pooey through the open doorway, slamming the doors shut behind them. He quickly sealed the doors with a beam of white light.

A deep growl echoed through the building again, shattering the windows at each end of the hall.

Kieron turned in the direction of the growl with his pulse racing as a giant claw burst through the floor, each talon on it the size of him.

"I'm not fighting that." Pooey shook his head. "Nu uh"

"You make a run for it, and I'll hold it back," Kieron said unsurely. He was pretty certain that he'd die, but he was determined to take responsibility for this. He had put them into this situation after all.

He gripped Lucian's arm. "Make me a promise. Find Dora and get her back home safely." He stared in earnest at the fallen angel.

Lucian sighed and shook his head. "Great, you're a fucking lemming. Come on." Lucian scooped up

Pooey on one arm and grabbed Kieron's wrist in the other before he ran, dragging them both towards the open window. Kieron ran with him, staring at the window in horror as he realized that Lucian planned to jump out of it. Unable to stop because of the momentum, Kieron yelped as Lucian jumped out of the window, taking them with him.

Kieron cried out as they dropped towards the ground, his pulse racing. He peered up at Lucian in horror. Was he trying to kill them?

The angel spread his wings, catching the wind and gliding through the air, holding Pooey in one arm, and gripping Kieron's wrist in the other as he swooped over the city.

Peering back, Kieron saw a massive leviathan's head poke out of the window behind them with ice snorting from its flared nostrils.

"Is it going to follow us?" he asked.

"No, dumbass. Leviathan's can't fly." Lucian panted a reply while scowling down at him.

"Why are we flying so fast then?" Kieron asked.

Lucian nodded down to the city that was rapidly illuminating below them as lights appeared in the many windows. "The army of pissed off angels that are being woken up, and you weigh a fucking ton. Would you like to try flying for once?" Lucian scowled down at him. "Or if not, perhaps you should eat fewer doughnuts."

"I don't eat doughnu—" Kieron paused as he realized that he had wings of his own. He quickly spread them as Lucian released him, flying up into the sky on his own.

He caught Pooey as Lucian dropped him too.

The little demon scowled up at Lucian. "You did that on fucking purpose." He narrowed his accusing eyes.

"What, can't ninjas fly?" Lucian's mouth turned up at the corners into a wicked smile.

Kieron stared down at the city below as it began to light up beneath them. "All the angels are waking up. We need to hide."

"Follow me. I know a place we can go." Lucian swooped down into a dark forest, winding his way through the trees.

"Why are we following that dick? He always takes us to the shittiest places," Pooey muttered.

"We need him. He can help us find Dora. I'm sure it won't be as bad a place this time."

"Yeah, right, assuming he doesn't drop me on my head first." Pooey clutched the folder in his hands, digging his little bear claws into the cardboard. "And it's not as if he's abandoned you before. Oh wait…"

Kieron frowned. Lucian might be his father, but he certainly wasn't someone he could trust. The man had left him to suffer in Hell for most of his childhood. When they'd first met, he'd shot him out of the sky and had his coven of witches torture him. Trusting the fallen angel to help them might not be the best idea. Pooey was right. Lucian hadn't given them many good reasons to trust him.

"WWDD?" Pooey asked, interrupting his thoughts.

"What?" Kieron frowned down at the brown fluffy demon.

"What would Dora do?"

Kieron considered the question. Dora was the one who'd allowed Lucian to come with them in the first place. She was also the one who'd kept him in line. Without her around, Lucian was taking charge, and that wasn't okay. "She'd bring him along, but she wouldn't let him take over."

Pooey nodded. "We need to stop letting him make all the decisions."

"Once we get to the hideout he's taking us to, we can find out where Dora is and call the shots from there." Kieron narrowed his eyes at Lucian as he flew ahead of them.

"Yeah, assuming it isn't another insane, angel nightmare," Pooey muttered.

7

HEAVENLY HORRORS

Dora shivered as she stumbled across the desert, guided only by the light of the moon. The expanse of nothing seemed to stretch on forever, but she rationalized that she'd only been walking for a few hours.

She couldn't help but panic every time she heard the wind rush over the wasteland. She was certain that the patrols from Camp Angel would be coming for her soon. In fact, she was surprised they hadn't shown up yet.

Maybe they don't know that I'm missing?

Tired of walking and feeling sore all over, she tried again to make her wings come out. Flying would get her out of here so much faster.

She dropped her bag on the dusty ground. Then she slowly exhaled, trying to summon her wings. She closed her eyes, trying to concentrate on her back.

Come on. Fly me the fuck out of here.

After a few moments of clenching all her muscles to try to push the feathered things out of her back, she sighed. She glanced back, shaking her head at the lack of wings. Clearly, her angel wings didn't come out on command.

Fine, I'll just walk out of here then!

She scowled as she reached down to pick up her bag, pausing when her fingers brushed over something brittle.

Glancing down, she yelped and jumped back, widening her eyes at the skeletal remains on the ground.

Snatching her bag up, she backed away and swallowed as she noticed an array of bones sticking up through the sand. Staring around her, it dawned on her that she was standing amidst a field of skeletons. She looked down at the one near her feet. Although just bone and dust now, she could make out a body with giant wings spanning out behind it from the skeletal remains.

Angel corpses... What the hell is this place?

Paying more attention to the bumps in the ground around her, she realized that she must have stumbled into some kind of angel graveyard.

Swallowing a bubble of panic, she threw her bag over her shoulder. Whatever this place was, she needed to go through it. There was no way in hell that she was going back to Camp Angel, and this was the only other option.

Just don't think about it. They're dead and long gone anyway.

She frowned as she stepped carefully around the bones before continuing on her way across the wasteland.

How can angels die anyway? Aren't they already dead?

Galvanized by a need to get out of here, she picked up her pace, ignoring the aches and pains in her tired muscles as she hurried over an incline. She hoped that once she reached to top of the hill, she'd leave this macabre place behind.

Forcing herself to hurry to the top, she eventually reached the summit panting for breath.

Remind me to do more cardio when I'm alive again. My fitness level sucks.

She frowned as she scanned the expanse of desert ahead. It was a circular enclave surrounded by craggy caves. On the ground were more angel corpses, but some of them still had skin on their bones.

With every essence of her being, she did not want to go down there. Every nerve in her body was warning her to turn back. But with nowhere else to go, she didn't feel as if she had a choice.

Hitching her breath, she froze when she saw movement out of the corner of her eye. Near the entrance to one of the caves, there was an angel bending over with his back to her. His wings were ragged and dusty, but the white feathers were still visible beneath the dirt.

Maybe he knows what happened here.

Even less eager to meet another angel, she weighed up her options. This angel was an outcast too. Maybe he could help her. Also, following this path without knowing what she was walking into seemed like a very bad idea.

At least I can find out what I'm walking into this time.

Gritting her teeth, she scurried down the hill towards the dirty angel before she had the chance to change her mind.

Goosebumps popped up on her arms as she silently stepped closer to him. She couldn't shake the feeling that there was something wrong here.

She stopped a few feet away from him, listening to the slurping sounds he was making.

Is he eating his dinner?

Her stomach grumbled.

I wonder if he'll share some with me.

She eyed his back. His robes were shredded and dark, hanging off him in tendrils as he hunched over something in his hands.

After deciding that her hunger was more important than her fear right now, she decided that her best option was to ask for help.

"Er, hey!" She called out to him, trying to ignore the feeling of impending doom.

His shoulders stopped moving as he froze.

Great, I've scared the shit out of hi—

She froze in horror as he spun around with blood dripping from his open mouth. In his hands, he appeared to be holding a disembodied arm.

Her stomach flipped over at the sight of the mauled tendons and raw flesh as the dirty angel swallowed what he'd been chewing. Bile rose in her throat at the thought of who or what he was digesting right now.

You've gotta be fucking kidding me, cannibals!

She stepped back, holding up her hands as a placation. "Never mind, I'm not hungry," she said as she backed away.

Chills trembled down her spine as his glowing red eyes locked onto her, and a deep growl echoed from within him. He dropped the bloody arm and stood up, a glint of hunger in his eyes.

Without waiting to see what happened next, Dora turned on her heel and ran.

Her pulse raced as she heard his heavy footfalls behind her. Too terrified to look back, she skirted around the bodies, trying to weave her way past the caves.

Her throat closed up in terror when another creature like the first one leapt out of a cave beside her.

Its hands clawed as it reached out for her.

Dodging sideways, she leapt over corpses, running from the creatures that were waking up in the caves around her.

I'm fucked! There' are too many of them.

Glancing back over her shoulder, her heart skipped a beat. They were lurching after her like mindless zombies, and they surrounded her on all sides. There was nowhere left to run.

Please, God. Make my angel wings work.

She closed her eyes for a moment, trying not to imagine what it would feel like to be eaten alive.

Why are there zombie fucking angels in Heaven anyway?

Her eyes snapped open when she felt her wings spread out behind her.

Thank you!

She flashed her wings, running forward and beating her wings to launch herself out of the graveyard. She rose up in the air above the creature as they reached out to try to grab her feet. She kicked them away, rising up into the clouds and leaving the horrific monsters behind her.

For a moment, she feared that they would follow her. Fortunately, these things didn't seem to know how to fly as they stood beneath her howling. She watched them for a while as they attacked each other for body parts. Then she turned and flew over the desert, hoping

to leave the memory of them in her wake.

What the fuck is wrong with this place? This isn't what Heaven is supposed to be like. Where is all the peace and tranquility?

DOWN THERE

"Oh, baby!" Pooey called out to the group of angels ahead of him, his hips swinging in a jaunty swagger as he made his way towards what looked like an angelic roadhouse.

Kieron shook his head at the little demon before he frowned at the bar. It was out in the middle of the forest with no other buildings for miles. It was a wooden shack in the wilderness, complete with neon signs and a group of scantily clad angels lounging outside the saloon-style doors beneath a sign that read:

HEAVENLY BODIES.

"What is this place?" he asked Lucian.

The fallen angel pondered the question for a moment, his expression confused as if he was trying to come up with a good explanation and failing dismally.

"Think of it as a slice of Hell that is tucked away in Heaven. If you want to do something bad, you come here."

"Is that allowed in Heaven?" Kieron frowned. It didn't look much like Hell to him.

Lucian shook his head. "No way. This place is off the radar. If the Angel Guard found out about it, it'd be shut down in an instant. They'd probably smite it out of existence."

As they reached the bar, one of the angels bent down to pat Pooey on the head. "He's so cute!" She stroked the little demon while cooing at him.

"Hey, hands off the fur. It's not free." Pooey brushed her away. "Cute." He spat out the word as he rolled his eyes.

"Omigod he talks!" She jumped back, a sparkle of excitement in her eyes. "I want one."

Pooey turned to face Kieron, his eyes like slits. "I hate this place."

Kieron sighed when he heard Lucian snort with laughter beside him. Anticipating another bout of fighting from them both, Kieron decided to head into the bar instead of listening to it.

He pushed open the saloon doors and walked into a room that did not meet his expectations. From the outside, the bar looked like a ropey old shack in the wilderness. However, inside it was a hive of metropolitan activity. From the stylish mahogany bar to the geometric artwork on the walls, every inch of the place looked designer.

Scanning the patrons milling around the place, some lounging in plush leather couches and others leaning against the bar, he noted that the clientele were all equally designer in their clothing.

"…Yeah, well you have flat-ass, and your—" He heard Pooey exclaim as the door swung open behind him, inviting a draft into the perfectly temperate room. The little demon was silent for a moment, but not for long. "Holy snazzy fuck!"

"Yes, that was the name they were going to go with, but Heavenly Bodies won in the end," Lucian muttered.

"Why, is it a whore house?" Pooey asked.

Kieron winced as a chubby little angel hurried towards them. He had a fat Cuban cigar hanging from his lip, and he wore a black suit that was straining around his rounded belly that was threatening to pop off the buttons.

"Lucian, my old friend!" The chubby angel cried as he rushed over, pushing past Kieron to give Lucian a hug. After kissing the Fallen One on both cheeks, he stood back and looked him up and down. "It's been too long. You've lost weight."

Lucian shrugged. "Hi Gale, how's tricks? I love the new look."

Gale turned around and clicked his fingers.

"Miguel, clear out the executive seats, now!"

Pooey shot Kieron a look of surprise, mouthing the words: 'what the fuck?'

Kieron shook his head.

"Come, come, mon ami. We shall drink and reminisce, no?" Gale gripped Lucian's arm and led him towards the bar. "And your friends are welcome too of course, come!" He glanced back over his shoulder at Pooey and Kieron, giving a command that caused them both to jump.

"This is gonna be interesting," Pooey muttered to Kieron out of the side of his mouth.

"What do you mean?" Kieron whispered back.

"Gale looks like the Godfather's cheerful younger brother."

Kieron studied the man as they followed him through the crowds of people, heading for the darker area at the back of the room. He was a jolly, chubby little angel. But the gaudy rings on his stubby little fingers, the suit and the cigar were all a bit gangster-like. "Maybe he just likes to dress that way."

"Yeah." Pooey nodded as the sarcasm dripped off his tongue. "I totally can't imagine him sticking a horse's head in my bed."

Trying to ignore the imagery that Pooey created, Kieron followed Lucian and Gale, wondering what nightmare his father was going to lead them into this time. At least no one was trying to kill them yet. It was an improvement on the rest of Heaven.

"Sit, sit." The little angel waved his hand at the table while puffing on his cigar as Kieron and Pooey reached him and Lucian, who were already seated in the plush booth.

Pooey and Kieron slid onto the opposite padded bench.

Kieron peered at their host, trying not to stare at the long scar across his cheek, but unable to look away now that he'd noticed it.

The gangster narrowed his eyes at Kieron.

Lucian cleared his throat. "So, Gale, I need a favor."

"What happened to yer face?" Pooey asked in a loud voice that caused Kieron to wince.

Lucian shook his head and closed his eyes in what looked like a moment of silent pain.

"What's it to ya?" Gale asked with narrowed eyes.

Pooey shrugged. "It looks cool. Was it an epic fight?"

Gale's moody expression lit up into a smile. "That it was, my little friend. I took on the Angel Guard, and I won."

"We're they trying to burn you for being a demon too?" Pooey asked.

"I went against my cast." Gale shrugged. "They don't like us to disobey."

"Anarchy, I like it." Pooey nodded with

admiration.

"When the cherubs don't fall in line, they take your wings," Gale muttered ominously.

"You were a cherub?" Pooey widened his eyes. "What like all harps and love and shit?"

Kieron tried to imagine Gale as a cherub, but he could only imagine him holding a machine gun during prohibition rather than pointing an arrow of love at someone's heart.

"It was a few lifetimes ago, but it's why I opened this place, a spit in the eye of the angelic regime we live under." Gale gestured around his bar. "We've come a long way from cheap liquor and dancing girls."

"You've done well, Gale. It's why I came here. The Guard are after us." Lucian leaned forward, lowering his voice. "We need your help."

"What do you need?" Gale narrowed his eyes.

"Sanctuary," Kieron said. "We need a safe place to stay while we find my friend."

Gale stubbed out his cigar in the golden ashtray, narrowing his eyes for a moment. "What kind of friend?"

"She's not an angel," Lucian quickly said.

"Then what's she doing here?"

"She's a human. Well, she migh—ow!" Kieron didn't finish as Lucian kicked his shin under the table.

"She's a human soul that they're trying to recruit into the guard. We just need to get her out before they convert her."

Gale smiled. "Fuck over the Angel Guard? Yeah, I'm in. Come on." He stood up and smoothed out his suit with a sweep of his hands. "I have the perfect army to help you." He turned on his heel and began walking towards a closed red door.

"What the fuck!" Kieron hissed at Lucian while rubbing his leg, which was still stinging from the kick.

"For fucksake, don't mention demons here. Even Gale isn't *that* open-minded," Lucian muttered out of the side of his mouth before he stood up and followed the other angel.

"Well, shit. There are racists everywhere. I was just starting to like the little guy too," Pooey grumbled as he slid out of the booth and jumped down onto the floor.

Kieron frowned. "We can't stay here too long. What if our horns come out?"

Pooey ruffled his fur. "Let's just find Dora, and then this nightmare will be over."

Kieron nodded before he stood up and followed the little demon.

As he reached the group, Gale tapped a code into the keypad beside the door before pushing it open and stepping inside.

Kieron followed Lucian and Pooey into the room, his eyes widening at the gloomy interior. It was a dark room containing hundreds of angels, who were hunched over computer monitors that emitted a dim glow across the walls.

Frowning, Kieron peered over the nearest angel's shoulder, studying the images and text on his screen. The angel appeared to be reading a story on a fanfiction website, which judging by the title was a pornography novel about One Direction called:

SOLD TO 1D IN AN AUCTION ON EBAY: A ONE DIRECTION SEX SLAVE DIARY.

The angel turned to look at him with a tear glistening in his gray eye.

"Is it any good?" Kieron asked.

The angel nodded. "It's so heart-breaking." He sniffed and wiped his nose on his sleeve before pointing to the screen. "When she says: *Lorna's POV: Harry did then take me from the behind, and I did scream out my luvs for hiz sexy ass, but I was all fifty-shades, bitches, and like tied up 'n' shit...* It's just so... so very human." The angel hugged himself. "So much emotion..."

"Right." Kieron nodded, trying to see something human or emotional in the story. Even for a boy from hell with a grandmother who was no stranger to whips and chains, he couldn't see anything romantic in the words.

He turned to Pooey, bending down to whisper in the little demon's ear. "What's a POV?"

Perhaps that is the romantic bit.

The little demon scratched his head for a moment. "Power of Vengeance?"

Kieron shook his head. That couldn't be the meaning.

Pooey peered at the screen for a moment. "Power of Vagina!" he said loudly, causing several angels to gasp and look up from their computers.

"Oh great," Lucian muttered before slapping his forehead.

The angels began to close their eyes and chant, some falling from their chairs and kneeling in prayer.

"Now they'll never help us." Lucian groaned.

"Why not?" Kieron stared at the room full of praying angels.

"That stupid ball of shit just invoked their penance." Lucian pointed to Pooey. "They'll be praying for fucking days now."

"I didn't do shit." Pooey scowled at Lucian.

"You said the unspoken word."

"Which word is that?" Kieron asked.

Lucian turned and narrowed his eyes at him. "I'm not going to fucking say it again. They'll pray for even longer!"

"Does it sound like vajayjay?" Pooey asked.

"Yes, and shut up for fucksake!" Lucian snapped.

"Why do they have to do penance if they mention the, er…" Kieron tried to think of another word for female reproductive anatomy that wasn't frowned upon by some culture or another, but he found it increasingly difficult to think of any word for vagina that wasn't a taboo. After going through the many words for female genitalia and unable to think of one that wasn't considered a bad thing for some stupid fucking reason or another, he eventually shouted out: "Down there!" while pointing to his crotch in an urgent manner.

"Down there…" The angels behind him chanted in unison, and he turned to find them touching their foreheads to the ground.

"Seriously?" He turned to Lucian. "What the fuck?"

Lucian shook his head as if trying to shake off the ridiculousness of the situation. "Well, we were going to get the angel hackers help in finding Dora because they were going to hack into the mainframe. However, since this little shit has just invoked a prayer of penance with his wonderful conversational skills, we're now stuck with working on the file on our own. Come on." The ex-angel stepped over Gale, heading for an empty desk ahead of them.

"Seriously, the *mainframe*?" Pooey cried as he followed him. "Are we gonna hack in through your backdoor too? Will you be bending over shortly?" The little ninja shot Kieron a look of disbelief.

"Yeah, keep talking, shit ball. That'll help make things worse." Lucian called over his shoulder.

"There's no need to be such a *cunt* about it," Pooey shouted back at him.

"Down there..." the angels all chanted around them.

Kieron sighed, hoping the file about Dora's whereabouts held more useful information than his companions did.

9

VILLAGE OF THE DAMNED

ora woke up and rolled over, moaning at the hard ground beneath her. Every muscle in her body ached. She frowned when she felt grass beneath her fingers. Then her eyes snapped open.

She tried to fight off the fog of sleep and remember where she was as she stared up at the sky through the treetops above her. The thick green leaves trembled in the light breeze as the sunlight filtered through them, shining down into the clearing. Memories of the night before came tumbling back.

With a shiver, she recalled that her arrival here wasn't as tranquil as waking up here had been. After the desert, she'd found this forest, which had seemed like a good place to rest. If memory served, she had actually crashed here in every sense. Her wings had given up from exhaustion, and she'd plummeted into this clearing, which had seemed a good place to sleep when she'd landed in it with enough force to create a small crater.

It was a safe place to rest. You're still alive, and your brains haven't been scrambled or eaten.

At the thought of the zombie angels, she hitched her breath and sat up. She glanced around her. Other than thick green bushes and trees, there was nothing else here.

Groaning, she pushed herself up off the ground and clambered out of the hole she'd made in the forest floor. She peered down at it with a shiver. It looked a bit like a shallow grave.

Luckily, the dark thoughts abated when her stomach rumbled. She picked up her bag and peered inside at the food tray. Apparently, gravy and mashed potatoes didn't travel well because it had all leaked out across the inside of her bag, and it didn't look very appetizing.

"Fuck," she muttered before dropping the bag on the ground beside her.

She knew she needed to find food and shelter soon. Scanning the sky through the trees, she turned around, trying to work out which direction to go in.

To her left, there appeared to be smoke billowing in the air. Although probably not a good sign, it was a sign of life.

And where there's life, there's food and shelter.

After a few moments of debating whether to take her bag or not, she shook her head and left the sack on the forest floor. Nothing in the bag was going to be useful now anyway.

She turned on her heel and headed through the trees towards the smoke. Whatever it was, it had to be better than zombies, right?

Shivering at the memories, she tried to shake off the feeling of doom, but it seemed as if doom was all that Heaven had to offer.

There's something seriously wrong with this place.

Brushing through the thick foliage, she scanned the horizon for hints about what she was walking into. As the trees began to clear, becoming sparse, she could make out a small village on the outskirts of the forest.

Little dwellings with thatched roofs pumped out smoke from their chimneys. The cobbled streets were home to all kinds of angels, street vendors and farmers. She hid in the shadows of the trees, watching them. They didn't seem evil, but knowing her luck, they were probably all a group of happy ax murderers.

Come on. It might be a nice place.

After debating it for a few seconds, she decided to keep herself hidden. She peered down at her white clothing. The Camp Angel prisoner garb wasn't going to do her any favors. It was bright white and almost glowed in the dark forest.

Scanning the village again, she caught sight of

washing hanging on a line at the back of some of the cottages. The forest bordered the back gardens, meaning that it would be very easy to steal some clothes without being seen.

Hunching low, she ran through the trees, ducking back occasionally to make sure nobody saw her. Panting as she reached the back of the cottages, she stared at her goal. She needed to cross twenty yards of open field to get to the clothesline.

Closing her eyes for a moment, she tried to motivate herself. Without giving herself time to change her mind, she dashed out from beneath the cover of trees and raced towards the laundry that was blowing in the breeze.

Breathing raggedly as she crossed the field, she scanned it for people, but no one was there. The first thing she ripped off the line was a dark red cloak, throwing it around her shoulders to cover herself. Next, she grabbed some black pants and a tunic, bundling them up in her arms.

She scanned the back of the cottage. No one was shouting or looking through the window at her, which was a good sign.

She saw a pair of mud-caked black boots on the black porch and quickly ran over and snatched those up too. After a quick scan of the area, she ran into the open barn and paused to try to catch her breath.

Did I get away with it?

She peered around the barn, her eyes widening. It was not a normal barn with hay and machinery. It was a stone structure, which was home to a forge with an array of weaponry hanging from the back wall.

Oh great, I'm ripping off the blacksmith.

Closing her eyes for a moment, she grabbed a dagger and a sword off the wall. Then she pulled down a leather knapsack and threw her bounty into it before throwing it over her shoulder.

Without pause, she fled the barn, racing back across the field into the forest. She ran deep into the woodland, only stopping when she found a clearing.

Leaning back against a tree, she dropped the bag off her shoulder and peered down at her cache.

At least I can travel in disguise now.

She eyed the silver handle of the sword that was poking out of the bag.

At least I have a weapon now.

Her heart was still hammering against her chest, so she exhaled slowly as she stripped off her clothes and pulled on the black pants and tunic. They were a tight fit, but she managed to squeeze into them by loosening the laces that held them together.

That blacksmith must be a tiny guy.

She tied the laces on the back of the bodice. After pulling on the boots—which were a little bit too big, but seemed to fit okay once she tightened the laces— she peered down the leg of one of them. They were knee high with buckles strapped across them. She slipped the dagger through one of the straps, securing it to her shin.

Next, she picked up the sword and stared at it.

Where the fuck am I going to put this?

She peered down at her outfit. There was nowhere to hang a sword. In the end, she dropped it into her bag, deciding to figure it out later.

It not as if you know how to use a sword anyway.

She pulled on her cloak, fastening it around her neck and pulling up the hood to cover her face. Then she picked up her bag.

Okay, I'm ready. I look like fucking Robin Hood, but I'm ready.

Gritting her teeth, she headed back towards the edge of the forest and peered down the cobble road that led to the village.

I'm just going to walk in and get some food.

She nodded, trying to convince herself that it would be easy.

I'll be fine, assuming it's not the Village of the Damned and no one tries to eat my face...

Keeping her head down as she wandered down the path, she tried to ignore the loud thumping of her pulse in her ears. She forced her breathing to remain calm, which was no mean feat since she was almost certain she was having an anxiety attack.

The closer she came to other people, the harder it

was to maintain a calm exterior. Cold sweat beaded up her back, and her throat was dry as she passed some farmers loading hay onto a cart.

"Good morrow to ya," one of the farmers called out.

She smiled and nodded at him as she passed.

Okay, so far, so sane.

She passed a woman selling pies, a fruit vendor and an old tavern. People milling around her brought a sense of both panic and peace. On one hand, she could become lost in the crowds. On the other hand, she was surrounded by angels, which never ended well for her.

Her stomach grumbled again as she passed a bread stall. Reaching sideways through her cloak, she snatched up a loaf and hid it under her cloak. Breathing a sigh as she passed by without incident, she slyly dropped the loaf into her bag.

Peering back over her shoulder, she realized that the stall owner hadn't noticed a thing. She'd gotten away with it.

Emboldened by her first success as a shoplifter, she stole an apple off a cart as she passed it, then a bottle of milk off another stall.

As she strolled down the main street, heading for what looked like the village square ahead of her, she considered stealing more.

She shook her head. She needed a place to stay, and this looked like a good place. No one was paying attention to her. But if she was caught stealing, she suspected that the natives wouldn't be so friendly.

Yeah, but you need money for a room.

She tried to think of a good way to get money as she reached the large crowd of people gathered in the village square. As she contemplated stealing the purses from the belts of people she passed, she wound her way through the crowds. Everyone was staring at the stage, and no one was paying attention to her.

I'll only take money from people who look as if they have too much.

She glanced at the stage and then froze.

Bound to a post was a burned corpse of what looked like an angel. Beside the smoking remains were two members of the Angel Guard, judging by their uniforms.

"This is what we do to heretics! We will not suffer for their sins!" One of the members of the Angel Guard shouted out to the crowds.

"Yeah!" A few of the villagers agreed.

Awesome, Psychoville.

Dora began to back away, out of the crowd.

"Bring the other one!" The angel on stage commanded.

Dora watched in horror as a young girl with wings was dragged onto the stage. She couldn't have been older than fifteen.

"Please don't!" she cried. "I didn't mean it!"

The red-haired member of the Angel Guard displayed no emotional response to her pleading cries. There was no empathy in him.

Dora sighed as she watched the girl being tied to the post.

The girl begged and cried about how she hadn't meant to use her wings while the crowds around them were calling out for the death of the heretic. Apparently, heretic meant an angel using her wings.

Fuck it.

Dora tried to summon her power—demon, angel, whatever. She'd have been happy with a shotgun right now. Her hand glowed silver, and a silver glove appeared on it, one with a tiny crossbow.

Oh, come on! I get the toothpick blaster again!

She peered at the magical weapon on her hand. Unlike the demon version, this one appeared to shoot tiny silver arrows rather than toothpicks.

Shaking her head, she lifted her arm and aimed the crossbow at the Angel Guards on the stage.

This is going to be fucking ridiculous.

She took two shots, one at each angel. Then she lowered her arm.

The little arrows whooshed through the air, over the heads of people in the crowd.

Shaking her head, Dora waited for the most pathetic rescue attempt in existence to begin.

The arrows hit both the targets, one in the neck,

and the other in the shoulder. The red-haired angel slapped his neck as if trying to kill a bug. Then he froze. His eyes widened for a moment. Then he exploded and splattered all over the audience in a shower of blood and guts.

Dora's mouth dropped open in horror when the remaining member of the Angel Guard also exploded into flying mulch.

Oh fuck, what did I do?

The crowds ran around her in panic, fleeing the scene and screaming about dark magic.

The girl on the stage, who now looked a bit like Carrie due to being washed in blood, peered at Dora with wide eyes.

"Help me!" She whimpered, tugging against the ropes that bound her to the wooden post.

Hurrying over, Dora quickly untied her before turning to head for the forest. Getting the fuck out of here seemed like the best overall plan.

She glanced back when she heard footsteps following her. The angel girl was hurrying after her.

"What are you doing?" she asked the girl.

"I'm coming with you."

"I don't think that's a good idea." Dora shook her head.

"You're my hero." The girl looked at her with hopeful blue eyes.

Dora frowned. "There are no heroes, not

anymore." She turned and hurried into the forest.

"Yes there are. There's you." The girl rushed up to walk beside her. "I'm Lillian."

"I'm a demon," Dora muttered, trying to get Lillian to leave.

"Awesome. Are we going to Hell?" Lillian smiled.

Shit.

"Probably somewhere worse," Dora muttered.

LETTUCE

After leaving Gale behind, Kieron had found a sense of peace. It had been a relief to set out again on the search for Dora, especially since Pooey had found shouting the word 'muff' was his favorite past-time at Gale's place, and it had caused the hacker angels to go into a constant state of penance.

Kieron inhaled the scent of pine as he walked through the thick forest behind Lucian, who was grumbling about them all being caught if they went this way.

It had taken some time to convince Lucian to take them any further. After searching through the file on Dora, Kieron had discovered that she had been sent to a place called Camp Angel. When he mentioned the place to Lucian, the angel's face had visibly blanched.

If Dora is there, I'm going. I don't care how

dangerous it is.

"So what is Camp Angel?" Pooey's voice shattered the tranquility of the woodland.

Kieron watched Lucian's shoulders bunch up from the back, his muscles tensing beneath his leather tunic. Although he couldn't see the angel's face, the tension came off him in waves.

"You won't understand how this is bad, but that place is Hell. It's a reprogramming center for angels. They either beat the sin out of you, or they wipe your mind, leaving a subservient vegetable behind."

"Why's it dangerous then if it's full of vegetables?" Pooey asked. "Like, if an angry lettuce attacked me, I wouldn't be scared. It's just a lettuce."

Lucian spun around with a look of disbelief in his eyes. "Are you fucking serious? Have you ever seen a two-hundred pound, blank-eyed angel coming at you with a sword?"

"Er, yeah." Pooey nodded.

Kieron frowned down at the little demon. "When?"

Pooey stared ahead. "Kinda now." He pointed to the trees ahead.

Kieron spun around to stare at the line of trees. His eyes widened when he saw a giant angel wearing golden armor charging through the woodland and heading straight for them. As Lucian had predicted, he had empty eyes with no life in them, which caused a shiver to shoot down Kieron's spine when those dead eyes locked onto him.

"Oh shit." Lucian drew his sword out of the scabbard at his belt while turning to face the monstrosity that was pounding through the forest towards them.

The ground shook as the angel neared them, his giant bulk causing a tremor through the earth each time his giant feet pounded against it, leaving a trail of small craters in his wake.

Kieron's pulse raced. He didn't have a weapon, so he flashed his wings, preparing to grab Pooey and fly away. He swallowed at the sight of the giant angel. It looked as if it could easily crush him in its mighty fists.

"No worries. I got this." Pooey brushed past him and walked ahead of Lucian, holding out his tiny fur paw at the angel, indicating it should stop.

"What the fuck are you doing?" Kieron gaped at the little demon. "Get back here."

Pooey glanced over his shoulder at Kieron. He looked so tiny compared to the behemoth that was stampeding towards him. "It's fine. I've had experience with mindless beasts."

Kieron gaped as Pooey turned back to face the giant. "Hey, large ass, hold on there. I have a question."

Lucian flashed a look of disbelief at Kieron.

Kieron winced back. He had a horrible feeling he was going to end up having to scrape Pooey off the floor after this. He tensed his muscles, bracing himself for the inevitable impact of being hit by a giant angel.

"I command thee to halt, giant fuckwit!" Pooey cried when the angel didn't stop.

The angel came to an abrupt halt a few inches away from the little demon, and it stared down at him.

"Okay, cool. You follow the old commands." Pooey paused for a moment to clear his throat. "Doest thou have a name?"

The giant angel inclined his head sideways, his dark glare changing to a look of confusion.

"Okay, let's not upset that single brain cell of yours. From hence forth, you shall be called Lettuce. Do you understand?" Pooey asked.

The giant angel slowly nodded at him.

"Great. So, er…" Pooey peered back over his shoulder at Lucian and Kieron. "Do you guys have any requests?"

Lucian stared at the little demon with his mouth hanging open. His sword fell from his hand. He appeared incapable of speech for a moment, which was a miracle all by itself.

"What do you mean requests?" Kieron asked unable to take his eyes off the giant angel, who was standing silently beside Pooey like some kind of monstrous sentinel.

"Well, he's a model eight brainwash." Pooey patted the angel on the knee. "He's not too bright, but he'll do anything we want. I guess some dick decided to use dark magic here, but they didn't read the manual."

Pooey peered up at the giant. "Raise me in thy arms."

The angel reached down and picked Pooey up, holding him on his giant palm.

"Great stuff, let's have a look here." Pooey peered into the angel's eyes before glancing back over his shoulder. "Yeah, he hasn't been registered, so we can keep him if we want."

"Keep him?" Lucian choked out the words, finally finding his voice. "He's a steroid-fueled monster!"

Lettuce expelled a low growl.

Pooey raised his hands up to the sky before he muttered a few words under his breath. After an audible popping sound, a puff of purple smoke materialized in the air above him.

Lettuce blinked. Then he peered down at Pooey.

"You can speak now," Pooey said.

"Yes, master," the giant angel said.

"What the hell did you just do?" Lucian asked.

Pooey turned around and sat down on the giant's hands. "Well, essentially I just turned him into our warrior. He's kinda awesome, huh?"

"Er, how do you know how to control brainwashed creatures?" Kieron asked unsurely. The fact that Pooey was enjoying this was more concerning than the giant creature whose hands he was sitting in.

"I was once enslaved to this voodoo master in Hell. It was a long time ago, but this is his spellcasting. I recognized it immediately. I guess the fail angels pirated it, but the dumbasses forgot to read the instructions. Once you make a braindead being, you have to register them. Until then, they're anyone's mindless beast."

"Can we give him his own mind back?" Kieron asked.

Pooey pondered the question for a moment. "That's a bit tricky. I'd have to find the original design and see what they did with his mind first."

Lucian narrowed his eyes. "So what are you planning to do with him, keep him as a pet?"

"Well, I can't just leave him here, alone in the forest like this." Pooey patted his new pet on the arm.

"Yes, you fucking ca—" Lucian paused as a scream echoed through the forest.

Kieron turned to face the sound. It was a female scream. His heart thundered in his chest at the sound. He recognized that voice. It was Dora's voice. He was certain of it.

Without hesitation, he set off running towards the sound. Hope and fear bloomed in his chest at the same time. She was here. She sounded as if she was in pain.

"No, Lillian!" Dora cried as she helplessly watched the

young angel run out from beneath the cover of trees, straight into the path of holy fire that was blasting down from the sky above. She studied the four members of the Angel Guard, who flew overhead and relentlessly attacked them.

The only safe place was under the cover of the trees, but it was as if Lillian had a stupid gene. She saw danger, panicked and then decided to run towards it.

Dora winced because she knew that she was going to have to leave the cover of the trees, which was the only thing protecting her from having her ass burned off by angel fire. She shook her head and then expelled a sigh.

You can't leave Lillian to die even if she is a fucking moron.

"Fuck it." Dora tensed her muscles and then launched herself out into the open, chasing after the young angel. She feigned left as a blast of white angel fire smashed through the trees beside her, igniting them in an instant.

As the trees around her blazed into a wall of fire, sweat beaded her brow. She hurried through the fiery copse, trying to avoid being burned as she chased after the young angel who was running straight into the path of the Angel Guard.

She glanced up at the Guard, who were circling above. Then she quickly jumped aside as another bout of blasts scorched the earth around her.

"Lillian, stop!" Dora shouted over the din of explosions and the loud beat of wings as she dodged one ball of fire after another. "It's not safe. Get back here, you idiot!"

Lillian glanced back at Dora over her shoulder with smudges of soot on her face. Glowing embers floated around her as the forest was ablaze and the ground shook with each new explosion. Her eyes were wide with fear as she shook her head and tears rolled down her cheeks, leaving clean streaks in the soot.

The sight of such helplessness caused a vice to clamp around Dora's heart. She gritted her teeth and lowered her head before charging through the flames to get to her new friend. Lillian might be a dumbass, but she was a good soul. Dora was determined to save her.

As she neared the angel, Dora held out her hand. "Come back to where it's safe."

Lillian shimmered as the flames surrounded her. She tentatively reached out for Dora's offered hand.

Then a blast of air blew Lillian's blonde hair over her shoulders as a guard swooped down and plucked her out of Dora's reach before he soared up into the sky with the young angel trapped in his arms.

"No!" Dora cried as she watched him fly away with her friend, watching in horror as the young angel struggled, helplessly captured in his embrace.

When Dora heard the beat of wings behind her,

she dropped to the ground on instinct, narrowly missing being captured herself by a second member of the Guard as he swooped overhead.

After rolling over, she scanned the sky. She could see Lillian hanging from the other angel's grip as he flew away with her. She tried to follow, but she had to duck down again as another member of the Guard took a second pass at trying to grab her.

When a fireball exploded into the ground beside her, she rolled sideways. Everything was happening too fast and all at once, and she realized she was trapped. There were two angels swooping down, trying to get her and the third was raining down angel fire, surrounding her in a blazing circle. There was nowhere to run, and Lillian was becoming a speck on the horizon as the fourth angel flew away with her.

Dora swiped sweat and soot out of her eyes. This wasn't the first time she'd been surrounded by violent assholes, and it wouldn't be the last. Snarling, she crouched down, preparing to attack. If she was going down, she was going down fighting.

She summoned every power inside her, demon, witch or angel, she didn't care what came out as long as it was strong enough to defeat these bastards.

She felt her wings growing and glanced back to see what kind she had. They were white and fluffy. She peered down at her hand, but the tiny crossbow had not appeared.

Oh, come on. If ever I needed a stupid toothpick to fight with, it would be now.

She shook her hand, trying to make her weapon appear. She realized nothing was going to happen after a few seconds of staring at the unmarred skin on her hand.

That's just great. I got selective powers. They only appear when they feel like it.

A whoosh of wings caused her to abruptly glance up. A mean-faced member of the Angel Guard was swooping down at her. She braced herself for impact, curling her wings around herself. With no weapon, she had nothing to fight back with.

When she heard a loud 'oof', she parted her wings just in time to see another angel ram into the guard who had been coming after her. The sight of peppered wings caused her heart to jump into her throat.

Kieron!

"Up and away, my monster-angel bitch!"

Dora turned her head to see a giant angel launch into the sky. She squinted to see what was riding on his back, and then widened her eyes when she realized it was Pooey riding a giant angel. "Oh, what the fuck?"

"Yes, those are the words my son has been waiting to hear from your lips. That's why he dragged my ass back to this shithole, to hear you say those three little words to him—*what the fuck.*"

Dora hitched her breath and spun around to find

Lucian landing on the grass behind her. "What?" She frowned at him. Since when did Lucian have a son?

"Shall we?" He indicated they should leave.

Shaking her head, she pointed to the horizon. "They took Lillian."

"They'll take us all if we stay here. They've probably already called for backup." Lucian shook his head. "Come on. We need to get out of here. You can't help your friend if you've been fried by holy fire."

Dora nodded. He was right. She couldn't help Lillian if she was vaporized. She launched up into the sky and then turned to see Lucian do the same. She waited for him to fly by before she followed him.

STOLEN KISSES

Dora searched the blazing forest for Kieron, and her heart skipped a beat when she finally located him soaring in the sky above her. She flew up to him, beating her wings as hard as she could.

He's here. He's really here.

She couldn't believe how she could feel happy at a time like this, but just the sight of him gave her hope. He was the light in her gloomy existence. Okay, he was a demon, but just being around him made her feel safe. After all the chaos in her life lately, he was the only thing in it that made sense to her.

His eyes lit up when he spotted her. He swooped down to her, cutting through the clouds to get to her. The only sound in the air was the loud beat of his powerful wings.

They collided in mid-air, and his arms wrapped

around her in a tight embrace as he hauled her against him. They tumbled in the sky, a spinning projectile of entangled limbs, kissing each other, holding on tightly as they soared above a lush green landscape.

"I missed you." She panted out the words between kisses, sinking into his muscled arms with a sense of relief, feeling as if she had come home. This was Heaven. This was what Heaven should feel like, love, warmth and safety.

"I thought I'd lost you." His voice cracked on the last word, and she pulled back to see pain in his eyes before he leaned forward and crushed his lips against hers in a kiss that seared her soul.

She kissed him back with just as much urgency. She thought she'd lost him too. She thought she'd lost everything that mattered.

"Watch out, you fucking morons!" Lucian's voice snapped her out of her lovestruck daze. She glanced ahead and hitched her breath. They were tumbling straight towards a cliff.

Hearing Kieron gasp, she looked up at him as he tightened his arms around her and flashed his wings to pull them back before they hit the side of a mountain.

The air whooshed around them as they pushed against it before finally coming to a halt a few feet away from the hard granite and eventually hovering in the air beside the giant mountain. Kieron swooped down to a narrow path on the side of the cliff, where he gently

deposited Dora before landing beside her and lowering his wings.

She caught her breath for a moment before peering up into his big blue eyes. There was a turbulent storm in them. "I—"

She didn't finish as he captured her in his arms again, pushing her back against the wall as his lips descended on hers, stealing her breath away and causing her pulse to race.

Losing herself to the rhythmic beat of her heart, the feel of his hard muscles pressing against her, she felt her skin burn at his touch.

"Oh, come on. Get a fucking room, will ya." Lucian's voice echoed behind her.

Kieron pulled back, breathing heavily as he rested his forehead against hers. They stared at each other in silence for a moment, catching their breath and trying to untangle, but unwilling to release each other.

"Hello, the Angel Guard, remember them? They're still chasing us. Now is not the time for teenage groping!"

Kieron looked up and scowled at Lucian.

Dora peered back over her shoulder to see Lucian smirking.

"Now son, Heaven homework first, then girls."

She narrowed her eyes and flipped off the fallen angel.

"And you really should pick a nicer girl," Lucian

muttered.

Wait a minute. Why is Lucian acting like a father? He doesn't have kids, does he?

She glanced at Kieron as his muscles bunched up, and he expelled a low growl.

Upon seeing his eyes darken in anger, she shook her head, silently telling him not to react. Obviously, Lucian was playing him, but she couldn't figure out the father and son connection.

"What the fuck are you doing just standing there?" Pooey's voice echoed through the clouds as he flew through them on the back of a giant angel. "Find somewhere to fucking hide!"

Blasts of angel fire shot through the clouds behind him.

Without waiting to find out how many of the Guard were chasing him, Dora grabbed Kieron's arm, and she dragged him into the opening in the cavernous rock beside them. Even though the dark cave was dank and cold, it was an improvement on being exposed.

She pulled Kieron against her as Lucian shot into the cave too, pausing to scan the darkness before he landed in the entrance.

He didn't stand there for long when Pooey shot into the opening on the back of a giant angel, knocking Lucian over and landing on top of him in a squashed heap.

Dora peered down at them as they scrambled to

get off each other, rolling to the side and jumping to their feet.

Lucian was the last to get up. He scowled at Pooey as he brushed dust off his pants and tunic. He opened his mouth to speak, but Dora shushed him as she peered around the corner of the entrance.

She hitched her breath when she stared outside.

The Angel Guard began to appear through the clouds, scanning the skies for their prey. Her eyes widened as more and more of the Guard appeared. There were hundreds of them. Clad in golden armor and armed with deadly looking weapons, they searched the skies.

She felt Kieron's arms wrap around her waist as his chin rested on her shoulder and his body pressed against her back, causing her pulse to race even more.

"What are they looking for?" he whispered in her ear, and she felt his hot breath brush against her cheek. "Me, I think they're hunting down me."

12
FALLING FOR AN ANGEL

Dora backed away from the entrance of the cave as another patrol of angels flew by it. Fortunately, they were unaware that their bounty was only a few feet away. She turned to face Kieron, Lucian and Pooey. "What are we going to do? We can't get out," she whispered.

Lucian scanned the cave for a moment. "We go through the mountain. It's the only way."

Dora frowned. "Through it, we don't even know if there is a way through it, and we have no light."

"I can light it up," Lucian said. He clicked his fingers, and they lit up with magic for a moment. "I was just going to wait until we were away from the entrance. As for the way out, we aren't going that way any time soon, so..." He shrugged.

She glanced at Kieron and Pooey, who both

nodded. Apparently, their trust of Lucian had grown since she'd last seen them all. She was still finding it a little bit difficult the trust the fallen angel.

Probably because he's been full of shit since I met him.

"Okay, let's do that." She indicated he should lead the way.

In a very unlike Lucian way, he stepped ahead of them into the darkness. She and Kieron followed him, leaving Pooey and the giant angel to take up the rear.

After a few moments, a dim glow lit up the cave when Lucian summoned a golden orb of light. When they turned the corner of the tunnel they were in, he clicked his fingers and the light expanded, becoming brighter and hovering above them like a small sun, lighting up the interior of the winding tunnel for them.

Dora studied the craggy walls of the mountain. They were dusty and cracked. The ground was uneven with dips and slopes that had been worn away by time rather than feet. They really were heading into the unknown.

"Where are we going when we get out of here?" Pooey asked, and his voice echoed down the tunnel.

Lucian glanced back over his shoulder. "Assuming we survive this god forsaken place, we're going back home through the same door we used to get here."

"You used a door to get into Heaven?" Dora turned to Kieron.

"Yeah, there was kind of one in your dad's church." Kieron smiled at her.

"So, we just walk through it, and we're back on Earth?" Dora felt a blossom of hope. She was going home! She frowned for a moment. "What about this angel stuff? I've got wings. I can't go home with wings!"

"You kinda had wings before," Pooey said.

"Yeah, but they weren't white and fluffy. Mind you, they were killing me." Dora sighed. That's what had gotten her into this mess. She'd been half demon, and it had been sucking the life out of her. That's how she'd died. "Wait a minute. Am I dead?" She widened her eyes.

"You looked kinda dead on Earth." Pooey nodded. "Don't worry. You get over it after a few hundred years of having a pity party."

"But I don't want to be dead. I just want to be normal again." She frowned.

"We can fix you. I'm sure of it." She felt Kieron's hand wrap around hers.

Lucian let out a long drawn out sigh ahead of them.

"What?" she asked.

He turned around and stared at her. "Oh, poor you. You're an immortal angel. How you must suffer. You've had mortality, demonic power and now you're a godly being. Woe is you!"

"Screw you. You've been trying to stop being an

angel since I met you!" She narrowed her eyes at him.

"Yes, and look how well that turned out. I'm stuck in fucking Heaven again because of *you*!"

She put her hands on her hips. "You didn't have to come here."

"Yes I did!" Lucian's nostrils flared in anger.

"Why?" She frowned at him. He was clearly upset about being in Heaven, but she couldn't figure why he'd come here in the first place. It wasn't as if they had bonded.

"Because my fuckwit son is in love with you, and he'd get his ass fried if I let him come here on his own!" Lucian threw his hands in the air before turning on his heel and storming ahead.

"Who's his son?" Dora asked, suspiciously eyeing the giant angel beside Pooey. "Is it that guy?"

"What, Lettuce?" Pooey asked with wide eyes.

"His name is Lettuce?" Dora gaped at the giant, who slowly turned his head to stare blankly at her.

"Yeah, I named him. It suits him, don't you think?"

"It does not fucking suit him." Lucian's voice carried through the tunnel as he shouted a response. "It's the most stupid bloody name I've ever heard, and that's saying something since yours is *Pooey*!"

"Don't you insult me or Lettuce! You're the one who named your unicorn skanky."

Lucian came to a halt. The muscles in his shoulders

bunched up as he slowly turned around and glared at the little demon with a storm in his brown eyes.

"Oh wait, I named your unicorn Skanky," Pooey said, displaying an impish grin.

Lucian expelled a growl.

"What? It's a great name for her. She likes it."

"So who is your son—?" Dora stared at Lucian, and her words trailed off. She didn't know how she hadn't noticed it before, different eyes, but the same glare in them, the same nose, the same jaw. She gasped and turned to face Kieron. "Is he your dad?"

"Apparently, he is my biological father," Kieron muttered.

"How is that even possible?" Dora widened her eyes.

"I'm thinking it was due to some Barry White and a magic overdose at one of those demon orgies," Pooey said.

"It was not an orgy!" Lucian cried.

"If you don't stop talking now, I'm going to kill you both." Kieron scowled at them.

"That's my boy." Lucian smirked at him.

"What was it, romance under the bleachers then?" Pooey asked.

"Oh please, we were both adults. It happened at a professional gathering." Lucian averted his eyes.

"So he was conceived on top of the office photocopier then?" Pooey turned to Kieron. "I guess your first baby pictures were printed by Xerox."

Kieron launched himself at Pooey, but Lettuce stepped between them before he could strangle the little bear, knocking Kieron back with a gentle brush of his hands.

"Okay, enough!" Dora said. "We have enough enemies without bickering between ourselves." She turned to Kieron. "Who you are isn't defined by your family or where you started your life." She offered him a hand to help him stand up. "I should know."

"But we always bicker. It's our bonding process," Pooey said.

She sighed at the little demon. "I think we're all bonded enough."

"I dunno. Lettuce hasn't been included much." Pooey shrugged.

She studied the giant angel. "What is Lettuce? Is he a giant?"

"Nah." Pooey nodded at him. "He's just an angel who got brainwashed.

Dora's blood ran cold at the words. That's what they were making in Camp Angel. That's what they were going to do to her.

"What is it?" Kieron asked, frowning at her.

"They were going to do that to me."

She shivered. Then she scowled. "What the hell is wrong with this place? This can't be Heaven. Lucian, this can't be how it's supposed to be."

Lucian scowled. "It's not how it's supposed to be."

"Then why is it so fucked up here?" She tried to remember all the religious things her father had taught her. Admittedly, he wasn't the best reverend in the world, but she vaguely remembered him mentioning Heaven in his sermons.

"Because no one appreciates a good creation. They always try to improve it, and then they fuck it all up. Why do you think I left?"

"But where is God? I mean, can't he stop this all from happening?" Dora asked.

Lucian threw his hands into the air. "Yes, let's blame the guy who created it. It's His fault that morons took over his life's work and shat all over it." He turned on his heel and stormed down the tunnel. "Are you coming, or shall I leave you here?"

"Ooh, someone hit a nerve," Pooey muttered.

Dora frowned at the back of the fallen angel. So there was a God after all. She reluctantly followed the rest of the group. She really did want to go home, but guilt gnawed at her. What would happen to the brainwashed angels? What would happen to Lillian?

Dora peered down the center of the massive atrium inside the mountain. The ground was hundreds of feet below them. She looked up to study the sharp stalactites that hung from the ceiling, which lit up as Lucian's

luminescent globe floated around them.

"It looks like we're flying down," Lucian said as he spread his powerful white wings and stepped off the ledge.

Dora watched him smoothly turn and swoop down towards the base of the cavern. His wings were golden tipped, and they spanned out far wider than hers or Kieron's.

Pooey went next, leaping onto Lettuce's back and commanding him to follow Lucian.

She turned to Kieron.

He smiled and released her hand before spreading his wings and launching himself off the ledge. Watching him hover in the air in front of her caused her pulse to race. With his short golden hair and tawny skin, Kieron looked the most like an angel, which was a bit ironic since he was half demon. His blue eyes sparkled at her as he smiled and held out his hand.

She smiled back and stepped off the ledge. Then she screamed.

Wings out, you fucking moron!

She dropped like a stone, and it felt as if her stomach had just jumped into her throat. Along with panicking that she was about to die for a second time, she was also busy berating herself for being so entranced by her demon boyfriend that she forgot to summon her fucking wings!

She saw Pooey's eyes widen in horror as she

dropped by him. She was pretty certain that her own eyes were pulling a similar expression. She tried to concentrate and summon her wings, but nothing happened.

Looking down, she realized she was heading straight for Lucian, so she aimed for his back as if she was skydiving.

He peered back over his shoulder, and he mouthed the words: 'oh fuck' before she landed on him, driving him down towards the ground. Luckily, he was only a few feet from the ground, so they didn't land too heavily, and he broke her fall.

Pushing her off him, he rolled over. "What the fuck?"

"Sorry, er, my wings didn't work."

"So why did you jump off the fucking ledge?" He stared at her as if she was insane.

Kieron swooped down and landed beside her. "Are you okay?" He knelt beside her, putting an arm around her shoulders.

"Is *she* okay?" Lucian gaped at him.

"I thought they were working. I'm sorry, I didn't mean to—"

"Land on my back with the force of a thousand obese people?"

"I'm not that heavy!" Dora stood up, brushing dust off her pants.

"She didn't do it on purpose," Kieron said.

"Son, your girlfriend just tried to ride me." Lucian stood up and shook his head.

Dora scowled at him. "Eww, no I didn't. I only fell off the fucking ledge because I was too busy staring at Kieron to realize that my wings weren't out…" She trailed off when she realized what she'd said.

Wincing, she peered at Kieron.

A satisfied grin curved up one corner of his mouth. "So, you fell for me."

"Shut up," she muttered, fighting a losing battle to hide her smile.

"Oh, I'm gonna be sick." Lucian turned away.

"Maybe it was a leap of love." Kieron stepped forward, brushing a strand of her dark hair away from her eyes.

"You fell off a fucking cliff because you were staring at a boy," Pooey said loudly behind them. "You're like a human lemming!"

Dora winced. Pooey was right. "Maybe it was vertigo." She shrugged at Kieron, trying not to notice the hurt expression on his face. They needed to slow down though. She was getting stupid, seriously stupid over him. "We need to get out of here."

She turned and frowned when she noticed Lucian lying on the ground ahead of them, pressing his ear into the floor. "What the hell are you doing?"

The fallen angel held up his hand, motioning for silence. After a moment, he stood up. "We need to go down."

"Why, what's under the mountain?" Pooey asked.

Lucian smiled. "The sewers."

Dora wrinkled her nose. "We're going into the sewers?"

Lucian nodded. "Yeah, and more importantly, we're going home."

THE GUILT TRAP

ora studied the silvery tunnel walls as she followed the rest of the group. For a sewer, it was kinda pretty.

She turned to study Kieron's back, which was also a nice view.

Her eyes wandered to the giant ahead of him, who was ducking down to shuffle through the tunnel. She had no idea what they were going to do with Lettuce when they got back to Earth. It wasn't as if a ten-foot tall angel could blend into the local community.

I hope we can get back there. What kind of door is in a sewer?

She shrugged. This was how the rest of the group had got into Heaven, so as long as the door worked both ways, she'd be home in no time.

Frowning, she tried to work out why that thought

didn't make her feel happy. She wanted to go home. That was all that mattered, but she couldn't shake the feeling that it was wrong. Her stomach was twisted into knots, and the unfamiliar feeling of guilt weighed on her.

I have nothing to feel guilty about.

She tried to shake the feeling, but it wasn't going anywhere. She experienced a nagging sense of shame over abandoning the other angels in Camp Angel. She felt bad for the angels who were being brainwashed, the people in the villages who were banned from embracing their angelic nature, over Lillian...

It's not my fault. I didn't make Heaven suck. It was this way when I got here!

She chewed her bottom lip in a moment of indecision. She knew what she should do. She knew what her conscience was telling her to do, but she didn't want to do it.

I'm going home. I can't stop an army of psycho angels anyway. I can't help them. I can barely help myself.

There was that unfamiliar guilt again, the feeling that she was lying to herself and making excuses to avoid what needed to be done.

She expelled a sigh.

Why do I always have to do everything? Can't I just go home this time?

She realized—as she tried to rationalize her own

selfish need to go home—that the reason she had to fight this battle was the same reason that she'd had to fight every battle so far. There was no higher power coming to save them. There was no one else coming to help these beings. If she wanted to see a superhero save the day, she had to become one.

It would be easy to ignore the suffering of others if she convinced herself that *someone* would help them. It was easy to pass on the responsibility by claiming it had nothing to do with her. But that guilt, that rotten feeling in her stomach was because she knew she was lying to herself. She couldn't go home yet. She had to help them, not because any of this was her fault, but because there was no one else to help them, because if she didn't help them, no one would.

"Shit," she muttered as she peered ahead.

The rest of the group were happily chatting instead of bickering for once as they hurried towards a large golden door ahead of them.

She dreaded telling them that they had to stay here, but she'd made up her mind. She was staying. She had to.

Just get it over with.

"Um, guys, hold on. Stop a minute." She winced. This was going to suck.

The group paused, and everyone turned to face her.

"What's wrong?" Kieron asked, a frown forming

on his face when he looked at her.

"We can't go home yet," Dora said.

"Why not?" Pooey asked.

"We need to help the angels."

"Say what now?" Lucian raised an eyebrow.

Dora tried to explain how she felt, but it was easier to think it than to say it to three incredulous faces. To be fair to Lettuce, he didn't look as if he cared either way. "Heaven's all fucked up. There are innocent beings here that need our help."

"Fuck 'em. Let their god help them." Pooey shrugged.

"If there is one," Kieron muttered.

"That's just it though. There isn't anyone here helping them. If we don't help them, who will?" Dora began to feel increasingly stupid as she said the words, but she also knew that she was right.

"So you want us to what, take on the armies of Heaven to save a couple of angels from ending up like Lettuce?" Lucian asked.

"Yes!" Dora nodded.

"With what?" Lucian asked.

"What do you mean?" She frowned.

"What exactly are you going to do to save the angels from these unstoppable assholes, who have the power of the universe at their fingertips? Which almighty force are you going to use to stop them, your sarcasm?"

"To be fair," Pooey said to Lucian. "I think your sarcasm is more toxic than hers."

"Not the fucking point. She couldn't even save herself!" Lucian pointed to Dora. "Like fuck I'm staying here for something so stupid. Why should we? It's not our problem."

"It is our problem!" Dora cried. "We're here. We've witnessed it happening. That makes it our problem."

Kieron inclined his head, deep in thought for a moment before he nodded. "Okay, I'm in."

"What?" Lucian cried. "If I walk past a homeless guy, is his welfare my fucking problem too?"

"It depends on if you're self-absorbed or not," Pooey said. Then he glanced up at Lettuce. "Okay, I'm in too as long as Lettuce gets his mind back from all this."

"You're all fucking nuts. You realize that you're demons and not fucking superheroes, right? You can't do anything anyway. The only thing you're going to accomplish is being blown into streaks of soot by angel fire. That's what's going to happen. Your masterful heroic plans will end with you all becoming shit-stains across the asphalt. Good luck with that." Lucian turned on his heel and began walking towards the door.

"Er, wait a minute," Pooey said, gesturing for him to come back.

"What, so you can convince me. No thanks."

Lucian rolled his eyes.

"No, that's not why," Pooey said, urgently pointing at the door.

Dora peered around Lucian at the golden door ahead. At first, she frowned, trying to see whatever it was that Pooey was pointing towards. Then she widened her eyes when the golden door rippled. "What the fuck is that?"

Lucian turned and studied the door. His shoulders tensed. "It looks like you get your wish after all." He began to back up.

"What is it?" Kieron asked.

"I could be wrong, but it looks like a trap to me," Lucian said, backing up.

Dora widened her eyes when the door rippled again, and then a figure stepped out of it as if he materialized out of thin air. With the gold paint camouflaging him, it took her a moment to recognize the angel. She hitched her breath when she did as Sergeant Fluffers opened his eyes.

He flashed a wicked grin in her direction as he raised his sword.

"It's a trap. Run!" she cried before she spun around to flee down the tunnel. But her voice cracked in horror as she saw members of the Angel Guard hurrying down the tunnel behind them.

She swallowed a bubble of panic, trying to think of a way out of this, but the sewer was small and cramped.

They were completely surrounded by the enemy.

Tensing her shoulders, she tried to summon her tiny weapons. When that didn't work, she pulled her dagger from her boot instead, glancing at Kieron as he flashed red eyes at her and his little horns poked up out of his head.

"You really shouldn't have gone AWOL, recruit," Fluffers said as he took a step towards them.

"I tend to disagree," Dora muttered as she eyed the Guard who were edging towards her with their swords drawn.

"Joining with demons is a death sentence." The sergeant's voice was a deadly echo down the tunnel.

She glanced back at him, frowning when she saw Lucian out of the corner of her eye. He appeared to be praying. He was looking down at his hands and whispering into them.

I suppose now is as good a time as any.

"Can you even die here?" Pooey asked. "I mean, like, aren't you already dead?"

Fluffers narrowed his eyes at Pooey. Then he glanced back at Dora. "Animating your teddy bear is also a sin."

"The fuck did he just call me?" Pooey cried.

"Seriously, it's a sin to bring your teddy bear to life?" Kieron raised an eyebrow.

Pooey narrowed his eyes at Kieron. "Can we please address the fact that I'm not a fucking teddy bear?"

Dora frowned at Lucian as a glow of light shone in his hands. "What are you doing?"

The fallen angel finally looked up, and she gasped. His eyes glowed gold as he raised his arms and a blast of light exploded from his body, surrounding them.

Fluffers and the Angel Guard were knocked back by the blast as it blew a hole in the roof above them, shooting a golden beam of light up into the sky and creating a large hole for them to escape through above.

"I'm letting you guys talk shit while I summon a tunnel of holy fire to create an escape route," Lucian muttered.

Around them, white flames kept the Angel Guard at bay, who were cowering back to save themselves from being burned. But inside, the air was glittery gold, a hazy sanctuary.

"What is it?" Dora asked, running her hand through the haze.

"YOU!" Fluffers bellowed from the other side of the flames.

Dora glanced at him to find him staring at Lucian.

"Yeah, I'm back." Lucian slowly turned his hand before flipping off the sergeant. Then he glanced at Dora and Kieron. "What are you waiting for, fly!"

Dora and Kieron both summoned their wings, nodding. She felt Kieron grip her hand before they launched up through the burning crater and flew out of the sewer and into the sky.

She peered back over her shoulder to see Pooey following them on Lettuce's giant back. For the first time ever, she began to worry about Lucian.

"What about Lucian? We can't leave him there," she cried over the wind as she and Kieron fled.

Kieron frowned as he peered back. "I think he'll be okay."

The golden tunnel of light exploded into a white flash that shook the foundations of the city, and a lone figure shot up through the earth.

She breathed a sigh when she recognized the fallen angel. He'd made it out, and he was heading straight for them.

"What are you fucking doing? Move it. They're coming!" Lucian cried.

14

HOLY HIDEOUT

Dora gasped as a loud alarm blared across the city. "What the hell is that?" She shouted over the din at Lucian.

"They're calling in backup. Fucking move it!" He turned in the air and launched forward, using his powerful wings to fly away.

Pooey went next on the back of his giant angel, and Dora and Kieron took up the rear.

Glancing back, she hitched her breath as an army of angels launched out of the windows of a nearby building. There were so many, they filled the sky.

Ignoring her racing pulse, she put as much power into her wings as she could, trying to emulate the same actions of Lucian, who was expertly darting through the clouds ahead.

She peered at Kieron. His powerful wings were

beating in the air too, but he was slowing every so often to match her pace.

He doesn't want me to get left behind. I'm slowing him down.

Feeling guilty for being the weak one, she tried to make her new wings flap faster, but that didn't seem to help. There was an art to it, she discovered. You needed to catch the wind, like a sail and glide through the air. Flapping around a lot wasn't going to help.

Once she got into the rhythm, it seemed easier to keep up with the group.

I've got it. This is going to work.

She flashed a smile at Kieron, but it slid off when she saw the worried expression on his face.

Peering back again, she almost swallowed her tongue. The army was so close. At the speed they were flying, they'd catch her in no time.

Gulping and trying to force herself not to panic, she determinedly stared ahead. Her eyes widened in horror when she saw a blast of white fire heading straight for her. She just about managed to narrow her eyes at Lucian, who was shooting holy fire in her direction, before Kieron's strong arm wrapped around her waist and hauled her against him and out of the way.

The blast of holy energy shot past her in a streak of white fire, blazing through the clouds and exploding into the army on her trail.

"Come on, we need to hurry." Kieron's breath warmed her cheek as he pulled her forward, gliding past Lucian.

"What are you doing?" Dora cried at Lucian, who was hovering in the air and shooting blasts of white fire from his hands at the oncoming army. She meant, why had he shot at her, but he clearly misunderstood.

"I'm saving your ass. Get the fuck out of the city, now!" He flashed a warning look at her before his brown eyes focused on the enemy as he summoned a ball of purple light in his hands. "Let's see how you like the darkness, bitches!"

Kieron released her, and they flew side-by-side towards the outskirts of the city.

"Won't he get caught?" Dora asked. Lucian was a bit of an asshole, but he seemed to keep saving them. It seemed wrong to leave him there, fighting an entire army on his own.

"Do we care?" Pooey asked as they glided past him.

"Yes," Kieron and Dora said in unison before pausing to shoot a questioning look at each other.

"Oh great, when did asshat join the inner sanctum?" Pooey pouted at them.

"He's helping us. That makes him one of us," Dora said, and she meant it for about three seconds.

"Aww, I get to join the fuckwit party. I'm so honored." Lucian's voice echoed behind her, and she spun around to find him smirking at her. Behind him, the sky was darkened by purple smoke, and the armies chasing them had gone.

Her instinct to tell him to fuck off was overpowered by her shock over the amount of power he had. He'd knocked an entire army out of the sky by the looks of it. She opened her mouth to ask him how, but he interrupted her.

"Come on. They'll regroup and be back in no time. Escape now. Insult later." He glided past, beating his wings as he flew through the white clouds ahead.

"What the hell?" Dora turned to Kieron.

He shrugged. "At least he's on our side."

Dora winced as the muscles in her back ached. It seemed as if they'd been flying forever over the City of Angels and across miles of farmlands after that. She gritted her teeth, trying to ignore her aching wings, but she knew she was going to have to stop soon.

She glanced back over her shoulder at the empty blue skies behind her. There was no one following them. It seemed that Lucian's purple explosion had put them out of action for now.

"Where are we going?" She called out to Lucian since he was leading them again.

"Home," he shouted back at her.

She frowned. They were following him to his

home, but they didn't really know that much about him. What kind of place did a being like him call home?

He's a warlock, fallen angel who shoots purple light from his hands that can blow up an army, and who happens to have a pet unicorn back on earth. Oh, and he's Kieron's father...

She tried to rationalize that none of them were particularly normal. She was a human girl, who wanted to be a witch, but had been turned into a demon, and now she appeared to have become an angel. Kieron was half angel and half demon, and...

She glanced at Pooey, who currently resembled an evil Care Bear.

Well, at least he's still just a demon.

Her eyes wandered to Lettuce. She wasn't really sure what he was classed as.

It was fair to say that they were all a little strange, and they were all more than one thing in some way or another, but something about Lucian nagged at her. There was some bullshit about him that she just couldn't ignore.

Why's he running when he has so much power?

"Oh you've gotta be fucking kidding me?" Pooey's voice snapped her out of her thoughts, and she glanced ahead.

They were heading towards an old mansion house. It might have been a palace once, one with sculpted marble pillars surrounding it and manicured gardens surrounding it. It wasn't one any more. Dark ivy crawled up the walls, which were smudged with dirty gray streaks. Cracked pillars littered the overgrown lawn beside the remains of smashed windows and tangles of weeds.

The roof appeared to have been blown away in places, leaving scorched tiles and gaping holes behind.

Dora eyed the ruins with a look of concern. "This is home?"

"One of them," Lucian said. "It might need some cleaning up, but we'll be safe here."

"It might need some demolition," Pooey muttered.

"If you want to stay out here and die, that's totally your choice." Lucian offered Pooey a smile before he swooped down to his shoddy palace.

Dora sighed. Her wings weren't going to keep flapping for much longer. She was exhausted. "It'll do while we figure things out," she said to Pooey.

"Yeah, assuming it's not haunted by dead assholes." The little bear wrinkled his nose.

Kieron widened his eyes in horror. "Why would you put that image in my head?"

"There is something seriously wrong with you. You know that, right?" Pooey shook his head and then pointed to the palace below. "Take us down to that dump site." He told Lettuce.

"I'm not sure I want to go down there now."

Kieron turned to Dora. "It sounds worse than the sewers."

She smiled at the innocent look in his big blue eyes. It didn't matter if they were in Heaven or Hell, Kieron never changed. He was always the most honest, brave and silliest part of her world. "Come on. I'm sure it'll be fine." She took his hand as they swooped down towards the old mansion house.

The dilapidated gates were broken off the hinges and spattered with dirt and grime, but upon closer inspection, Dora found they were made of pearl. She frowned.

These are the pearly gates.

They stumbled up the long driveway, which was a muddy bog, full of potholes and weeds.

As they approached the large house, she stared up at the ramshackle building. It had been white once, but now it was faded yellow with dark stains down the stone and old vines crawling up it. Spooky didn't even cover it.

She jumped when the second story window burst open, and crows flew out of it. A pair of yellowing net curtains blew in the breeze for a moment before Lucian appeared in the window.

"Get out of my house, you fucking vermin!" he shouted at the birds. Then he peered down at her and Kieron. "Come in. It's perfectly hospitable. You can see your inheritance," he added while looking at

Kieron.

She peeked at Kieron and saw him wince.

With a sigh, Kieron nodded. Then he took her hand, and they walked towards the front door. "This is going to suck," he muttered.

NO MORE HEROES

Dora listened to the unending squeal of old hinges as Kieron pushed open the front door to reveal the inside of Lucian's mansion. The interior was just as ropey as the exterior with cracks running up the pale walls. Dirty smudges were ingrained into the white marble, making it dingy gray and thick vines burst out of the tiled floor, climbing their way up to the roof.

She felt Kieron's hand tighten around hers as they walked across the threshold. Clearly, the place had been very beautiful once with statues and detailed engravings in the stone. Most of the paint had cracked off the ceiling, but she could still make out an angelic mural above them on the parts of the ceiling that hadn't eroded away.

The upholstery had mostly rotted away, leaving

dusty old rags instead of curtains.

They both jumped at the sound of heavy footsteps, turning to see Lucian bounding down the sweeping staircase ahead of them. He looked so excited that for a horrible moment, Dora thought he might slide down the marble banister.

Instead, he stood above them and smiled. "So what do you think of your new home?" He proudly spread his arms, obviously seeing something far grander than what they were seeing.

"It's a broken-down, old shithole," Pooey said as he stepped into the building behind them.

Lucian's jubilant expression was rapidly replaced by a scowl. "It just needs cleaning up."

Kieron ran his fingers over the dust on the mantel beside him. The ledge crumbled under his touch and fell off the wall, smashing into the broken tiles below it. "It er, needs a bit of work."

"You're all so fucking negative!" Lucian narrowed his eyes at Dora. "What about you? What do you think of it?"

"Are we safe here?" she asked.

"Yes. There's a boundary spell on it. Anyone who looks at it will only see—" He paused. Then he slapped himself on the forehead. "That's why you're all so fucking weird!"

"Wut?" Pooey said.

Lucian held out his hands and began muttering into

them. A golden glow grew in his palms into a ball of light. After a moment of more muttering, he turned his palms and shot the balls of what looked like sunlight at them.

Dora widened her eyes as one of the blasts hit her and Kieron, knocking them both onto their backs. Blinded for a moment, she rubbed her eyes.

"What the fuck…?" She pushed herself up onto her elbows and opened her eyes, widening them as the broken ruins seemed to repair around her, transforming into a gleaming white palace. The features were the same, the same staircase, the same ceiling, but they were new and in immaculate condition. It was the room of a god.

"What the hell was that?" Pooey jumped up off the gleaming white tiles.

"There's a protection spell over this place. I gave you immunity to it, so you could see what was actually here." Lucian folded his arms. "Is it still a shithole?"

Pooey peered around. "That depends entirely on if you have food in here, cheesy puffs would be preferable."

"Do you know how many carbs are in that shit?" Lucian asked.

"Do you know how many carbs are in this?" Pooey raised his middle finger and flipped him off.

"I always knew that carbs came from Hell," Lucian muttered.

Kieron turned to Dora, and he leaned over and whispered in her ear. "Let's go somewhere else. I can't handle another Lucian and Pooey argument."

She nodded, and they slowly stood up and slipped through the doorway beside them.

"Yeah, but they taste so sweet. Maybe you should *eat me!*" Pooey's voice echoed through the doorway behind them.

They silently hurried through an opulent sitting room where the furniture was covered by white dustsheets. They didn't speak, but seemed to be in silent agreement that they needed some time alone.

Dora smiled when Kieron's hand tightened around hers as they headed for the next open doorway. Her eyes wandered over to him. He seemed older, but then she supposed he was now. His shoulders were broader, his blue eyes a little bit less innocent.

How do demons age anyway?

She and Kieron had been in Hell for months before their time on Earth and then here in Heaven. She wasn't entirely sure how much time had passed during her jumps from dead to alive, but it had to be a few months, maybe even a year.

Am I seventeen now? Do corpses age?

As they hurried through another doorway, this time out into a conservatory, Kieron turned to frown at her. "What's wrong?"

She took a moment to wince at the bright sunlight

that was beaming through the glass doors of the conservatory. "Oh, it's nothing. I was just thinking about all of this."

She pushed open the door and studied the beautiful garden outside while enjoying the rays of sunshine that warmed her skin.

"This as in the house...?" Kieron trailed off as he pulled open the second door and stood beside her. "It is a very pretty garden."

Smiling, she rested her head on his broad shoulder. "It is, but I was thinking more about if I'm actually dead this time."

He wrapped an arm around her waist and pulled her closer. "You're not dead, Dora-minx. You're just in limbo."

She peered up at him. "Don't you have to die to get to limbo though?"

He shook his head. "I don't know, but you're no more dead than you were when I took you to Hell."

"I did wake up in a coffin after that though." The more she thought about it, the more it made sense that she was already dead. "I mean, how many people go to Hell and come back alive?"

"Do you think I killed you?" He turned to her with wide eyes. "I didn't mean to!"

"No, don't be silly..." She trailed off with a frown. "I don't know."

Kieron walked out into the garden, pacing and

shaking his head. He was clearly upset by the thought. "No, you were alive. You were alive on Earth because the matriarch killed you, so Hell can't have—"

"So I'm dead now?" she asked.

"No, well, your body maybe, but not *you.*"

"So I'm a spirit?"

"I don't think so. You're kind of an angel." He grimaced. "We need to fix that. It's not very attractive."

She narrowed her eyes at him. "Yes, that's the important part, how attractive I am."

"Exactly, as a demon you were much more appealing, but I liked you as a human too. I mean, this is okay." He waved his hand in the general direction of her body. "But when those wings come out…" He wrinkled his nose.

Scowling, she put her hands on her hips. "My wings are the same as yours! You realize that you are half angel, right?"

"I know. It must be quite grotesque for you. I'm trying to get rid of them though." He sighed.

Dora's mind flashed back to a tawny chested Kieron, flying to save her with his powerful white wings spread out, and the muscles in his arms and chest tensed. The image caused her pulse to race with excitement. "Not really. I kinda like it." She managed, trying to rid her mind of the evocative imagery.

He shot her a surprised look as if he thought she was nuts, which he probably did. Kieron had grown up in Hell. He thought angels were disgusting, so he hated being one.

She'd grown up in a church as a rebellious preacher's daughter, but even the Goth girl within couldn't deny the fact that angels were kinda hot.

Frowning again, she tried to understand the nagging thoughts in her mind. She tried to put them into words to make some sense of them. "If we're in Heaven now, and we're both angels, does that mean that God is real?"

Her whole life, she'd never believed in God, religion or anything her father told her. Now faced with the reality of Heaven, she had to address her own skepticism.

"Well yeah, we're at his place." Kieron shrugged. "It doesn't mean he's not a dick."

"He might be able to help us."

"That'd be a first," Kieron muttered.

She nodded. It would be a first, and she was still finding it difficult to accept. Dark magic and demons were so much easier to believe in than some almighty being who planned for everything to be this fucked up.

She wandered out into the garden, taking a seat on an old stone bench that overlooked a large pond. "Heaven's too fucked up for God to be real. Surely, he'd sort out the angels if he was good."

Kieron took a seat beside her and stared across the pond. "Who said he was good?"

Peering at him, she pondered the question for a moment. "Well, the bible."

"If someone wrote my biography, do you think I'd allow them to make me look like an asshole in it?" He shrugged.

She stared across the pond, deep in thought. After happy Hell and an insane supernatural Earth, she couldn't help but wonder what Heaven would turn out to be. Judging by what she'd seen so far, it seemed decidedly evil with all the brainwashing, cannibal angels and the burning of anyone who disagreed. "Maybe all the theology is propaganda. Maybe the good guys lost."

The thought was sobering, depressing even. But that's how it all looked. When you stripped away the history and the stories, all that remained was the fact that someone as good as Kieron came out of Hell, and that Heaven only had suffering to offer.

"Who are the good guys?" Kieron asked.

"That's what I want to know," Dora said.

16

ANGELIC INTERROGATION

After Kieron had gone to find some food, Dora decided to hunt down Lucian. Mulling over Heaven hadn't led to any epiphanies, so she figured she'd ask someone who was actually from here.

With determination, she stormed through the mansion house, looking for him. He wasn't going to bullshit his way out of giving her the answers this time.

No, but he's probably going to try to.

She couldn't help but admire the intricate carvings in the décor as she swept down the long hallway. From the coving to the picture frames, everything was carved with swirls and patterns. The paintings on the walls were unseen masterpieces, depicting angels and Heaven.

How does a guy like Lucian end up living in a place like this?

From what she knew about him, which wasn't much, he was a fallen angel, which meant he'd been thrown out of Heaven at some point. Although, his version of the story was that he escaped Heaven and threw himself into limbo.

She hurried down the long hallway, running her fingers over the balustrade beside her and occasionally glancing over it at the floor below. The house was huge, so finding Lucian was a bit like finding a needle in a haystack.

The sound of a violin echoed ahead of her, causing her to pause. Since neither Pooey or Kieron listened to classical music, she assumed it had to be Lucian.

The sound of music was ahead of her, so she followed it to a large oak door, pausing outside the room and listening. The orchestral music echoed hauntingly through the door in a beautiful melody.

She frowned. Lucian didn't seem like the kind of person who would listen to beautiful melodies.

Frowning, she gently pushed against the door, surprised as it slowly swung open to reveal a parlor. The room was light and airy with bright sunlight beaming through the open window as the white curtains wafted in the soft breeze.

Lucian lounged on one of the plush white couches. Beside him was an ornate sideboard that was home to an ancient gramophone. His eyes were closed as the enchanting music sang out of the golden horn of the device and filled the room with its enchanting melody.

Dora studied the fallen angel in silence for a moment while he was unaware of her presence. She'd never seen him like this before, serene, relaxed and almost angelic.

After a moment, she stepped into the room. Angelic or not, she still needed answers.

"Ahem." She cleared her throat, and his eyes shot open.

When he noticed her, his shoulders tensed, and he abruptly sat up and turned off the gramophone, scratching the needle across the record in his haste to silence it.

"You don't have to stop it. It's beautiful music." She winced at the sound of the needle scratching the surface of the disk.

"What do you want?" He turned to face her with angry brown eyes, clearly trying to cover up his moment of music appreciation.

"I want to ask you some questions about Heaven."

He shrugged. "It's full of psychos. What else do you need to know?"

Trying to form the words that would encompass the million questions she had was quite the challenge, but she decided that direct was the best way to go. "Where's God?"

Lucian averted his eyes. "Who says there is one?"

"But—" She paused, widening her eyes. Was he

saying that God didn't exist?

After a moment, she narrowed her eyes. This was still Lucian, and he was full of shit most of the time. "The bible says he does."

"Harry Potter says that wizards are real too. Have you met one?"

She studied him. "Well, there's you."

He widened his eyes in horror. "How dare you. I'm no wizard."

"You were a man-witch on Earth." She shrugged.

"Warlock, it's warlock, you foolish girl. God, can't you tell the difference?"

"What's the difference between a wizard and warlock?" She put her hands on her hips.

"Well they're....they're..." He paused for a moment. "Wizards are more..." He frowned as if trying to come up with a good reason. "Warlocks are badass!"

She rolled her eyes and took a seat on the chaise longue opposite him. "I'm not here to talk about warlocks."

"Then why are you here? Are you getting a teenage crush?"

"What the fu—"

He held up his hand to silence her. "I realize that I'm an overwhelmingly attractive man, but I could never do that to my son. You're a sweet kid, bu—"

"Eww!" Dora interrupted. "This doesn't have to

do with…Eww, that's not why I'm here!"

"And yet, you saunter into my private rooms wearing tight leather pants and looking hopeful," he muttered while shaking his head.

Dora glanced down at the leather pants she'd stolen off an angel's washing line. "These are all the clothes I have. I did not wear them for you."

He smirked. "I dunno. I've seen the way you look at me…"

She narrowed her eyes. "With disgust."

"The lady doth protest too much, methinks." He flashed a knowing smile, which made her want to slap it right off his face.

"First, I'm not a lady. Second—and I realize being an old fart that this might be news to you—women speak the same language as men do, so I say what I fucking mean."

Lucian gasped. "I don't look old, do I?"

Dora studied him. He didn't look old. He looked about twenty-five, but that didn't change the fact that he was old, and he looked too old for her. "You look your age." The corner of her mouth turned up. "What is that, two thousand years old?"

He narrowed his eyes. "You're so full of shit."

"Right back atcha."

"See, we're perfect for each other. But it's a forbidden love, so you'll just have to leave. Go now, before we're driven by our impulses." He raised an eyebrow and pointed to the door.

"Go fuck yourself." She stood up, intending to storm out of the room. But then she paused. "Motherfucker," she muttered under her breath before turning back to face him. "You're just trying to make me uncomfortable, so I'll leave you alone."

"I don't know what you mean, but if you keep standing there looking at me like that, I won't be responsible for my actions." He shot her a smoldering glance.

"If you come anywhere near me, I won't be responsible for my actions." She picked up a nearby candleholder and tested the weight of it in her hand. It was heavy enough to give him a headache.

"Just leave before I do something you'll regret."

"Tell me what I want to know, and I'll leave you alone." Now that she realized his whole act was about diverting her from the truth, she wanted to know what he was hiding even more.

He stared at her in silence.

"I'm not leaving until you answer my questions, and this romance bullshit can end right here since we both know it's bullshit."

He scowled and folded his arms. "I just think you have a problem with me because I see that you're not the right girl for my son. He can do better."

Dora tightened her fist around the candleholder. She knew this was just another attempt at making her leave, but he was hitting some nerves this time. When it came to Kieron, she had emotions, fears, love. "God, you're like a fucking internet troll. Can you stick to the subject, or is that too difficult for your tiny brain?"

"What, the subject of your slutty attempts to woo me or the subject of my son's welfare? I'm perfectly in my rights to be concerned by all of this." There was a wicked glint of light in his eyes. "You've always been a bad girl, am I right? Maybe you're just not good enough for Kieron."

She frowned, trying to ignore the words, but... Kieron was really good, and she'd never been very good at anything. Maybe he was right. A lump appeared in her throat. She was just a dead girl. There wasn't much she could offer Kieron. Even if she was alive and back on Earth, it didn't mean they'd end up together. Kieron was going to go back to Hell at some point. They were from different worlds, and in the end, this adventure wouldn't last. "I don't want to talk about that," she muttered.

"Oh, now that *you* don't want to talk about something, we have to stop because the world revolves around you, right?" Lucian threw his hands up into the air.

"Screw you! I love Kieron, and I'd never hurt him, unlike you! You're just a loser. What kind of father are you? You didn't even know he existed! You don't even know if God does!"

She dropped the candleholder onto the tiled floor and put her hands on her hips. "You're right. I don't need to talk to you. You don't know shit about anything. I thought that perhaps you might know more about Heaven, but that's unlikely since you've been blinded by having your head permanently up your own ass since the day you were born."

"I know more about Heaven and Earth than you ever will, little girl." He pointed his finger at her.

"Oh yeah, where's God then? Do you know that? I didn't fucking think so."

"I know what happened to him." Lucian looked indignant. "I'm just not telling you."

"Oh wait, you know a secret, and you're not going to tell me it? Are you five? Is it the secret with your imaginary friends in it?" She mocked him, inwardly relieved that her anger seemed to have removed any doubts about herself, and it had put the conversation back on track.

"I know what happened to God because I was fucking there!" Lucian shouted. "He created all this, Heaven and Earth, and then people complained. Everyone complained, so he fucked off and left." Lucian was pointing his finger at her with every word, his eyes blazing with anger. "I know because before he left he told me that creating something awesome was a wonderful gift, but the responsibility of maintaining it was a fucking nightmare! He left because he didn't want to end up doing customer support for the rest of his fucking eternal existence!"

Dora widened her eyes. It was a shocking revelation, but for the first time ever, she believed Lucian. He genuinely looked upset. "Shit really? That's why He left?"

"You try answering a million complaints about stupid shit like why camels have humps or why grass is fucking green. Inane whining got rid of God."

Lucian's story was pretty convincing. People complained a lot about everything, and most of it was inane shit that was completely pointless. "So that's why Heaven's like this, He left?"

"Yeah, he fucked it all off and vowed to never return. That's why Heaven's like this. It's run by the pieces of shit that nattered him away." Lucian shook his head in disgust.

"That's why you left. He was your friend."

The fallen angel nodded. "That's why I left."

"So, God can't help us get home." Dora sighed. She'd been hoping that divine intervention would be the answer.

FINDING GOD

Lucian looked thoughtful for a moment as he studied her. "Exactly, now get lost."

She raised a questioning eyebrow. "Wait a minute. If he's real, we can find him."

"If the dude doesn't want to be found, you won't find him." Lucian shook his head.

"If a girl from Berkville can summon a demon, why can't she find God?" Dora put her hands on her hips. "The angel doth protest too much."

"I want you to leave me in peace." Lucian ground out.

"I want you to help me find God!" Dora raised her voice. How difficult was it for him to just help them all get home? "You want to get out of here too, don't you? This is the only way!"

The door burst open behind her, and she turned to see Pooey walk into the room. He held a bag of cheesy puffs in one hand and one of the orange corn snacks from it in the other, which was hovering near his open mouth. "Is God even real?"

"Oh fucking great. The Scarebear is here," Lucian muttered.

"Lucian knows God, but he reckons we can't find him." Dora told the little demon.

Pooey popped the cheesy puff into his mouth and munched it thoughtfully for a moment. After swallowing it, he raised his eyebrows. "Why don't we just start looking where he was last seen?"

"Because he's not there," Lucian muttered.

"Yeah, but maybe he left behind some clues to his whereabouts." Pooey shrugged.

"Are you two just stupidly optimistic to annoy me? You cannot find God!" Lucian raised his voice.

"How do you know if you haven't looked?" Pooey asked as Kieron burst into the room behind him.

"Why would you want to find God?" Kieron widened his eyes.

"He might be able to send us home," Dora said.

"He won't help demons." Kieron shook his head. "This is not a good idea."

"Thas ma boy," Lucian said. "Listen to the voice of sanity."

"You know that He made demons, right?" Pooey

said before popping another cheesy puff into his mouth.

"No, that was the Devil." Kieron shook his head.

"And who made him?" Pooey asked while spitting out some masticated cheesy puff in the process.

"Er…" Kieron paused for a moment before continuing. "I can't remember anything else from Religious Education."

"Hell education is worse than the human one." Pooey shook his head. "What was the devil before he was the devil? I'll give you a clue." He pointed to Lucian.

"He was my father?" Kieron widened his eyes in horror.

"Lucian is the devil?" Dora asked.

Pooey slapped his forehead. "For fucksake, the Devil was a fallen angel!"

"Ohh right, yeah I remember that bit." Dora nodded.

"Do I still get to be the Devil in this charade of stupidity?" Lucian asked as he folded his arms and smirked at Pooey.

"You can be poster-child for all the cosmic mistakes in the universe for all I care, Lucy." Pooey flashed him a grin, his tiny fangs glinting in the light. Then he turned back to Dora and Kieron. "So yeah, the point is that God is fucking powerful. If we can find Him, He probably can fix everything and send us home. I didn't think he was real. But if shitbag over there knew him, then he's real enough."

"So what, you suggest that we just wander around looking for the creator of the universe, and he'll appear?" Lucian scowled at Pooey. "Sure, it's not as if angels have been looking for him forever or anything. Maybe, you're like one of those rednecks, who believes that God is speaking to them. Do you hear voices, little demon stain?"

"By angels, do you mean the brainwashed ones or the sadistic psycho ones, who have about as much vision as a blacked out window?" Pooey shook his head. "When are you going to get it through your thick skull that we're demons, man? Demons find shit that no one else can see all the fucking time. Demons can kick angel ass anytime and anywhere, so it's on bitches. We're going to find God."

"Yeah." Kieron nodded. "I'm in. Where do we start?"

"Oh well, have fun. I'm not a demon, so I'll just stay here." Lucian narrowed his eyes at them.

"He knows where God was last seen." Dora pointed to Lucian, which earned her a scowl from the fallen angel.

"It looks like you're coming too, Lucy." Pooey winked at him.

"I am fucking not. I'm not a demon remember." Lucian's eyes darkened with anger.

"It's okay, you're a clue. Plus, if you don't come

willingly, I'll have Lettuce carry you." Pooey glared at him.

The mood in the room changed as the two stared at each other before Lucian eventually broke the stare. "This is fucking ridiculous."

"Welcome to my life," Dora muttered.

"I don't want to be in your life. I want to be in mine, sitting on Earth with a beautiful coven fawning over me because I'm the most powerful warlock in existence. But no, you fucking rejects had to turn up and ruin everything. Now, I'm stuck in this fucking place again, and you're making me hunt down God." Lucian ranted with his eyes locked on Dora.

"Dude, they weren't beautiful witches. They were old hags using glamor on themselves. Now, be a good clue and give us some fucking information. Where did you last see God?" Pooey asked.

"Jesus fuck, fine!" Lucian threw his hands into the air and expelled an exasperated sigh. "This is going to sound insane, but he was last seen at God's Grotto."

"God's Grotto, what is he, fucking Santa?" Pooey asked.

"Shit, not that guy again," Kieron muttered.

Dora shot a sideways glance at Kieron. "You've met Santa?"

Kieron winced. "I might have er… Look, it wasn't my fault, and everyone gets presents now, so it's a good thing, right?"

She smiled at him. "What's he like, Santa I mean?"

"A greedy, fat bastard who eats people," Kieron muttered.

Dora widened her eyes. "What?"

"Nothing, it's just… a long story." Kieron nodded and expelled a sigh.

"Oh do tell, it's not like we're going anywhere," Lucian said.

"Where is God's Grotto?" Pooey interrupted.

Lucian's expression became a scowl. "That's the fun part. It's on the other side of the Golden Road. Good luck getting there."

Dora didn't like the sound of the Golden Road since golden things in Heaven had a tendency to explode, but she didn't like the sound of staying here for all eternity either. "Screw it. We can fly. Let's go to God's Grotto."

18

DON'T KICK THE ROCKS

K ieron was glad they'd decided to walk for most
of the journey and leave Lettuce behind at
Lucian's house. The giant angel did stand out
a bit, and Kieron was still a bit embarrassed by his white,
feathered wings. He was still a demon lord. Okay, he'd
been thrown out of Hell, and apparently, he was half
angel, but that didn't change who he really was.

He shot a sideways glance at Lucian, his father,
trying to come to terms with the fact that *that* guy was
his dad. The demon father he'd grown up with hadn't
been perfect. Lionel Lascher was no saint by any stretch
of the imagination. He couldn't help but wonder where
Lionel was now.

Does he know that I'm not his son?

He scowled and kicked a pebble. He'd always been
a disappointment to Lionel, never quite evil enough for

the lofty lord of Hell. Were these angel wings the reason why? Had he known that Kieron was someone else's kid?

What about Grammy, does she know I'm not her grandson?

It was depressing to think that the family he'd grown up with weren't his family. He'd never really been like them, but it had been comforting to be part of their clan.

He clenched his hands into fists. His great family hadn't been around when he was thrown out of Hell. They hadn't tried to find him.

They don't care about you, so why do you care about them?

Maybe because I'm a fluffy fucking angel.

He kicked another rock off the side of the road.

"Stop kicking the bloody rocks." Lucian's voice invaded his thoughts.

He turned to glare at him.

My new father and his awesome advice.

Kieron kicked another rock out of pure spite. "Why should I?"

"Because you'll piss them off." Lucian shook his head.

Kieron widened his eyes. "Are you nuts? They're rocks!"

"They don't like being kicked. The last thing we want to do is attract Mother Earth's attention, or worse, wake up Henge. Leave the rocks alone." Lucian rolled his eyes at him.

"You're so full of shit." Kieron narrowed his eyes and then rebelliously kicked another rock.

"Oww, motherfucker!" A tiny voice squeaked from the gravel road beneath his feet.

Kieron's mouth dropped open as he stared down at the rock he'd just kicked.

The tiny cracks in it formed into an animated expression of a scowl as it glared up at him. "Yeah, I'm talking to you, dickwad."

"Oh, great! Thanks, son. Thanks for pissing off the fossils." Lucian's voice grated on Kieron's nerves. In any other situation, he'd feel guilty for kicking another lifeform, but being around his real father was making him want to rebel, and nothing else seemed to matter. So he bent down and picked up the rock, holding it up to his face.

"You can shut the fuck up unless you want to skim across that lake." He pointed to the large body of water that was visible through the reeds on the left side of the path.

"Why are you talking to a rock?" Kieron heard Dora's voice behind him, and an inkling of guilt crept into his thoughts. Judging by the size of the rock, it was only a baby, and he was being mean to it when he really didn't want to be.

The rock's scowl creased up into sadness before it

opened its tiny mouth and wailed. "Paaaaaaappaaaa!"

"Holy shit!" Dora said as she peered down at the rock.

"Oh shit," Lucian said at the same time as he peered at the lake.

Kieron stared at the lake as the water rippled. The ground beneath his feet began to shake, and he stumbled as a giant monolith burst up out of the water and turned to glare at him.

"Who dares touch my son?" The ground shook as a deep voice echoed through the valley. The giant monolith turned to stare at Kieron, the dark cracks of its eyes narrowing when they saw what he held in his hand.

"The angel did threaten to drown me, Papa," the little rock in Kieron's hand squeaked.

"I didn't mean—can rocks drown?" Kieron asked the little rock. Then he widened his eyes as a dark shadow loomed over him.

He looked up to see a giant stone fist heading towards him.

Lucian sighed behind him. Then he stepped in front of him holding his hands up in submission. "Now, Henge, just because my son is a fucking moron, that's not a good reason to crush him."

"Lucian, is that you?" Henge paused and stared down at the fallen angel. "Did you shrink?"

"No, I think you just got bigger. All grown up

152

now, huh? How's the family?"

"When they're not being threatened by—" Henge peered around Lucian to look at Kieron. "Really, you have a kid, and that's him?" The mountainous creature sounded amused and surprised at the same time.

"He's mean, Papa!" the little rock cried.

"You need to toughen up, kid." Henge told his offspring.

"Wut?" The little rock blinked. "I'll tell Mama!"

"Fuckin' kids," Henge muttered. "Fine, you wanna play in the chalk pit again?

"Can I stay there all day?" The little rock looked sly for a moment before pulling an innocent expression.

"Yeah, if you don't tell your Mama, you can stay there all week!"

"Will you kick the shit out of this guy for me?" the little rock asked.

"What? No! Chalk pit or nothing, that's my last offer."

The little rock scowled at Kieron for a moment.

A bead of cold sweat rolled down Kieron's back. The little rock was so cold and calculating, and it looked as if it wanted his blood.

After a moment of contemplation, the little rock's expression broke out into a beaming smile. "Okay, Papa. I'll be a good rock if you let me play in the chalk pit all day."

"Thank fuck." The monolith lowered his giant

hand and opened it so that Kieron could drop his offspring into it.

"Are we there yet, Papa?" The little rock asked as the craggy monster held him carefully in the palm of his hand.

"No. We're having a grown up conversation. We haven't even set off yet." Henge shook his head at Lucian. "Kids, eh? So, where ya been? I thought you died."

Lucian opened his mouth to speak, but the little rock spoke first.

"Are we there yet, Papa?" Its voice was shrill and sharp.

"Long story," Lucian eventually said. "Maybe another time—"

"Waaaa, I wanna go now. You promised!"

"Ye, a boy's night maybe, we can relive the glory days." Henge had to bellow to be heard over the screaming infant in his hand. He looked a little bit desperate for a boy's night.

"Yeah, if the missus doesn't kill you, and the Angel Guard don't kill me, count me in," Lucian shouted.

"ABUSED CHILD! I WANT CHALKY!"

"The Angel Guard are after you again?" Henge shouted his question, trying to ignore the din of screaming coming from his offspring.

Lucian nodded.

"Aww, man, I miss those days. They're back over

the ridge, looking for…you, I guess."

"We better get moving then," Lucian shouted back. "Thanks. Good luck with, er, that." He nodded at the little rock.

Henge nodded. "I hope he grows out of it soon." The giant monolith said before he turned and waded across the lake, taking the wailing noise with him.

"That kid's got more evil in his little ridges than I have in my whole body," Pooey muttered as he removed his hands from his ears.

"Yeah, I should feel lucky that mine is just an idiot," Lucian said as he faced Kieron. "Don't kick the fucking rocks. Let's get out of here before the Angel Guard turn up."

"Which way?" Dora asked.

Lucian pointed to the left fork in the road. "We need to get onto Golden Road."

"Awesome, will we be going to see the Wizard?" Pooey asked.

"Yeah, you can be fucking Toto," Lucian muttered.

GOLDEN ROAD

Dora glanced at Kieron as he walked by her side. He'd been quiet and moody since their encounter with Henge and his evil offspring.

She studied Kieron in silence as they followed a bickering Pooey and Lucian. Kieron's blue eyes were narrowed as they focused on Lucian's back. Then sadness crossed his expression as he looked away with a sigh.

His eyes fell onto her, and he smiled. She smiled back and curled her fingers around his hand on instinct, holding it. Sometimes she forgot that he'd been dragged through Hell and back too. He hid his disappointments too well, but she'd seen him suffer all kinds of parenting nightmares since she'd met him. It couldn't be easy. Now with Lucian as his father and being stuck in Heaven, this probably felt like Hell to Kieron.

He squeezed her hand, slowing his pace, so that the gap between them and Lucian widened.

She matched his pace. It seemed as if he wanted to talk, and they hadn't had much of a chance to.

"Are you okay?" she asked quietly.

He nodded, but his expression remained grim.

She missed his permanent optimism. Where was the cheerful demon she'd first met? "Do you want to talk about it?"

"What would you like to talk about?" He frowned.

"You look unhappy. I thought maybe…" She nodded at Lucian, who appeared to be threatening Pooey, judging by how many rude hand gestures he was making at the little demon.

"No, it's…" He shook his head. "It's stupid."

"I like you when you're stupid." She smiled.

His frown deepened.

"I didn't mean it in a bad way." She winced. Clearly talking about feelings wasn't her gift. She decided to stick to what she was good at instead, saying things that most people found offensive. "I just wondered why you had a face that resembled a cat's ass."

"What?" Kieron widened his eyes in alarm.

"Kind of like this." Dora scrunched up her mouth into a sullen pout.

Kieron burst out laughing, and his blue eyes lit up with that light she loved to see in them.

She impulsively hugged him, relieved to see him smiling once again. Ever since they'd been in Heaven, he'd looked so much sadder than normal. She could only assume that it was something to do with the revelation that Lucian was his father.

Kieron's arms wrapped around her and tightened, drawing her close against his chest. His shirt smelled of clean washing, which was oddly comforting in such a strange place.

Heaven wasn't anything like what she'd expected, but then Hell hadn't been either.

"It'll be okay," she mumbled into his chest. "Fathers are never very normal."

He tensed in her arms. Then he pulled back and frowned down at her. "What?"

"Well, Lucian, he's what's bothering you, right? Don't worry about it. My father isn't exactly a saint either."

His frown deepened. "Lucian kind of is a saint, or he was. What are you talking about?"

"Er, about what's making you unhappy."

A confused expression appeared on his face. "What, you think Lucian is making me unhappy?"

"Well, that seems to be what's happening, yes." She nodded.

"He's a dick, but so was my last father. That's not why I'm upset."

She frowned. "Is it being in Heaven?"

158

"Well, that does suck, but no. It's you."

The words hit her like a brick in the face. She released him and stepped back. It was a shock to her entire body that was causing her eyes to water and her throat to burn.

Did he just say that I'm the thing that's making him miserable?

"What?" She had to force out the word. Through this completely ridiculous nightmare, Kieron had been the only constant, sane, wonderful thing in her life. Losing him now seemed like Heaven's worst punishment.

"Well, you make me upset now, so I'm trying to make that go away." Kieron frowned. "It's difficult."

Dora felt as if she was dying on the inside, but she refused to show it.

Now is not the time to cry like a little girl.

She scowled at him. "Okay, I know how to make it go away." She turned on her heel and stormed down the path towards Lucian and Pooey. She heard him calling out behind her, but she ignored it.

I'm a fucking idiot. I fell in love with a demon. What did I expect?

A little voice in the back of her mind cried out that it expected more than this, but she fought to ignore it. She wanted to go home more than ever now. It felt as if her world was falling apart around her, but she ignored that too.

Go home. Forget about all of this and just go home.

As she caught up with Pooey and Lucian, she noticed the sparkling golden road ahead of them. It shone with gossamer lights illuminating off it. Pooey and Lucian didn't seem to have noticed it because they were immersed in a fully-fledged, shit-talking battle as they stepped onto it.

"If I'm Toto, you're fucking Dorothy!" Pooey snapped.

"No, I'm the Great and Powerful Oz, and you're my bitch, so roll over and play dead!" Lucian cried.

Jesus, how long have they been having this argument for?

Dora watched them in awe as she followed them onto the Golden Road.

"We're off to see the wiz—" Lucian began, but he was cut short when Pooey jumped up and slapped him across the face, leaving a red mark on his cheek.

Pooey grinned.

Lucian's eyes darkened as he summoned a purple ball in his hands and stared down at the fluffy demon.

"No wait, what are you doing?" Dora cried as Lucian launched the ball of purple energy at Pooey, who tried to dodge it. But he was too slow, and the energy hit him squarely in the chest. He was knocked back, and he landed on the golden cobbles.

Dora was about to rush over to Pooey when she

saw him sit up and smirk at Lucian.

"That was just fucking lame. It didn't even tickle," the little demon said.

With a knowing grin, Lucian folded his arms as a rubber band materialized in front of Pooey.

"What the fu—" Pooey was cut short as the band pulled back and twanged forward to slap him in the face. "Oh very funny." He scowled.

"It will be." Lucian's grin widened as the band pulled back and twanged Pooey in the face again, and again, slapping him faster and faster each time.

"Oh you mother fuc—ow!" Pooey covered his face with his paws. "What the fuck? This shit is over-vengeful."

"Will you fucking stop it?" Dora narrowed her eyes at Lucian.

"Why should I?" Lucian shrugged.

"Because it's ridiculous." She ran over to try to stop the elastic band, only to get a nasty whap across her wrist for it.

Pooey narrowed his eyes before he vanished, leaving the band twanging fresh air.

Dora widened her eyes. "What happened to him?"

Lucian widened his eyes too. "I don't fucking know." He turned around, scanning the road.

Dora watched a large branch rise up behind him before it whacked him on the ass with a loud thwack.

"Oh you invisible, little shit," Lucian muttered

while rubbing his backside as he spun around.

Dora heard the patter of tiny footsteps across the cobbles as Pooey stalked Lucian in ninja mode.

She sighed. Then her heart froze in her chest as she heard Kieron's voice behind her.

"What's going on?" He sounded so normal, and that was the worst part of it, the lack of emotion in every word.

She turned away from the group as tears filled her eyes.

No, like fuck you're going to cry now, during this ridiculous fucking nightmare.

"I can't handle this shit right now," she muttered before she hurried down the road alone, leaving Pooey, Lucian and most importantly Kieron behind her.

"Oh, come on. It's only mucking around," Pooey called after her.

She couldn't explain to him what was happening inside her, so she just kept walking. Distance would make it better. She just needed to cry a little bit without anyone knowing. Then she'd be okay.

She stumbled as her eyes filled up with tears. The ground seemed to sway beneath her, and she stumbled forward, falling onto her knees.

She tried to stand up before she realized that it wasn't the tears making the road blurry. The road ahead was shimmering because it was moving!

Glancing back, her heart thudded against her chest.

Kieron, Pooey and Lucian had jumped back off the road as it rose up and down in waves like an ocean.

"What's happening?" she cried.

Lucian frowned at the rippling path. He must have said something because she heard Kieron shout: "It can't be what?" at him.

Lucian looked up with a panicked expression on his face. "I think it's reacting to the fighting! We must have activated the alarm system." He shouted out to Dora. "Hold on to something!"

The road began to crumble away beneath Dora as the cobbles bounced up and down, knocking her around like a rag doll. "What the fuck does that mean?"

"It means that—" Lucian's voice was drowned out as the road fell away between them with a loud crash, leaving a gaping black hole that appeared to have no bottom.

Dora clung to the shiny cobbles, but they were slippery and falling away like dominos. It wasn't long before she was hanging helplessly over a dark void, her hand gradually slipping off the few stones that remained.

"Angel Siberia, that's where it drops you," Lucian cried. "Get your fucking wings out and fly, now!"

Dora glanced back at him. She tried to summon her wings, she really did. But the second that she saw Kieron, her heart dropped and an overwhelming pain of loss filled her, which made her too useless to summon anything.

She closed her eyes as her hand slipped from the cobble, and she began to fall. She dropped like a stone, only seeing flashes of things as she fell past them. The look of horror in Kieron's eyes was the last thing she saw on solid ground.

EMOTIONAL ABYSS

The fall seemed to go on forever as Dora dropped towards an endless pit of darkness. She hugged herself, trying to summon her wings, but nothing happened. Closing her eyes, she hoped that it would be painless. Whatever shit happened next, she didn't want it to hurt.

She yelped when someone's arms wrapped around her, hauling her against them as she jerked in the air and began to rise. She didn't dare look back as she heard the beat of wings.

It'll be Lucian saving me, just like it was Lucian who saved me from the fire. That's why Kieron didn't save me. I'm so stupid. I should have noticed it then. He doesn't want to save me anymore.

Swallowing the painful knot in her throat, she turned to thank Lucian. He wasn't so bad after all.

Her eyes widened when they met Kieron's blue ones. He looked angry as he flew up, his wings beating hard to pull them out of the abyss. Golden rocks were falling around them as the road continued to crumble away above them, causing him to jerk sideways to dodge being hit.

"What were you doing going off on your own?" he snapped at her.

Dora felt the pain fade away as anger inflamed in her chest. "What the fuck do you think I was doing?" She scowled at him.

"I don't know, but you're not doing it again." His arms tightened around her, almost painfully crushing her against him.

"You can't tell me what to do!" she cried. Enough was enough. If he was going to break her heart, like hell she was going to be taking orders from him.

"Yes, I can. I can tell you what to do when you're so stupid that you keep on dying!" he shouted.

"Why do you even care," she muttered.

He clenched his jaw, his eyes on fire. "Because you left me before, and I'm not going to let you do it again."

Dora looked up at him and frowned. "Huh?"

"I'm not losing you again." He leaned down and kissed her before she could say another word, his lips angrily crushing against hers in a kiss that sent shooting sensations through her entire body. She helplessly clung to him as his strong arms crushed her against him. It

wasn't just a kiss. It scorched her soul. It was absolute possession.

She panted for air when he pulled away, staring down at her with that same fire in his eyes.

"I-I don't understand." She tried to get her head around the events of the day, but none of his actions made sense to her.

"I promised myself that I'd never let you go again. After you died... I'm never feeling that way again. You're going to be more careful." He squeezed her tightly as if to make his point. "You're not dying again, Dora-minx. I won't allow it."

"Ohh." She widened her eyes. That was what he'd meant by she was upsetting him. She hadn't realized, but he must have watched her die on Earth. It wasn't lack of love. It was too much of it.

She threw her arms around his neck and kissed him again, her heart jumping with joy. He was still her demon boyfriend. He did care if she lived or died.

He let out a low growl as they spiraled in the air, entwined in a heated embrace. "Never letting you go again." His low voice sent shivers of excitement down her spine.

She clung to him, her heart pounding.

I'm never letting you go either.

"Kinda wanting to barf up here." Lucian's voice called down to them.

"I second that motion." Pooey's voice followed a

few seconds later.

Kieron kissed her one last time. Then he reluctantly pulled back, resting his head against her forehead with his eyes closed.

She ached for him to kiss her again, but she sighed too before peering up at Pooey and Lucian, who stood in a similar stance side-by-side with their arms folded. Apparently, Kieron and her kissing was the one thing that could unite them in a kind of mutual disgust, judging by their expressions.

"Okay, enough of the gawping. We're—" Dora didn't finish as something yanked on her ankles, almost ripping her out of Kieron's arms.

She gasped and stared up at him with wide eyes.

He tightened his grip on her, pulling her back against him. The muscles bulged up in his arms before he yelped. "It's got me too!"

Then they were ripped downwards at high speed.

Dora looked down in horror to see nothing but smoke wrapping around her legs, but something was pulling her and Kieron down.

He was flapping his powerful wings, but the force dragging them into the abyss was far stronger than him.

She tried to free her legs, but the iron grip around her ankles was immovable. "What is it?"

"I don't know!" he cried as he tried again with no luck to free them both.

"Use your fucking wings." Lucian bellowed from

above.

Dora gritted her teeth and tried to summon her wings.

No you murky fucking smoke monster, you won't take Kieron away from me!

Her anger swelled in her belly, which she expelled with a cry as her wings shot out of her back. Forcing herself to concentrate, she beat them against the fast moving air, slowing their descent as Kieron joined her beating his wings in time.

They locked eyes, both concentrating on each other as they fought against the smoke that was dragging them down.

Dora breathed a sigh when Lucian appeared, flying beside them and gripping both their hands before he yanked them up out of the pit, tearing them from the smoke's grasp.

Instantly freed, Dora widened her eyes when she realized how much more powerful Lucian was. The speed at which he flew and how he easily broke away from the grip of the force inside the abyss were both revelations to her.

They cleared the chasm where the road had once been before he dropped them onto the grass beside Pooey.

She rolled over and stared at him with narrowed eyes. "You're so strong?"

Kieron scowled at her.

She shook her head and patted his hand. "I didn't mean it like that. I mean..." She turned back to Lucian. "How come you're so much stronger than we are?"

Lucian looked away for a moment. "What? I dunno." He shrugged.

"Yeah, you do." She scowled at him. There was something off about him. There had always been something off about him, and it was becoming more evident here in Heaven.

He waved away the question. "I'm older. Power grows with age, and all that shit."

"Bullshit," Pooey said. "I'm older than you are."

"No, you're not," Lucian muttered as he started walking away.

GOD'S GARDENS

"So how old are you?" Pooey asked, bristling with indignation as he smoothed the fur on top of his little demon head.

"That's a very rude question," Lucian said.

"I want to know the answer to that too," Dora said. "And I want to know where the hell we're going."

"Since you broke the Golden Road, we need to go through the Emerald Garden. It's going to fucking suck. Thanks for that." Lucian called over his shoulder as he led them towards a dark jungle of trees.

"I didn't break the road. You said it was an alarm." Dora scowled at his back.

"The alarm only goes off if there are volatile emotions on it. You looked pretty volatile." She saw Lucian's shoulder shrug.

"What about you and Pooey. You were pretty

volatile on that road. *You* were the one who set off the alarm!"

Lucian was silent for a moment. Then he nodded. "Yeah, it could have been that. Okay, so when we get to the Emerald Gar—"

"Hold on there, your wobbliness, how old are you?" Pooey interrupted before Lucian could change the subject again.

"That's none of your business." Lucian began walking faster towards the jungle ahead.

"I'd like to know how old you are too," Kieron said.

"Fucking hell!" Lucian stopped and spun around. "Fine! I'm older than time. There you go. Now give it a rest. We don't have time for this crap right now."

"What the hell does that mean?" Dora put her hands on her hips and scowled at him.

"Do you want a literal translation of every word, or—" Lucian didn't finish as a blast of holy fire exploded into a shrub beside him, igniting it into a burning bush. After he jumped sideways, he rolled over and stared at it for a moment in silent contemplation before jumping to his feet and turning to the group. "Run!"

Dora stared up at the sky, shivering when she saw the Angel Guard above. There were only three of them so far, but more were cresting the horizon, hundreds of them were flying in their direction in the distance.

"Fine, but if that bush starts speaking to me, I'm going to—" Pooey didn't finish as a blast of holy fire exploded into the ground beside them. He jumped sideways before looking up at the angel who'd shot at him. "Your aim is shit!" he cried before running into the thick copse of trees ahead.

Dora and Kieron quickly followed, stampeding through the thick jungle to escape the Angel Guard.

She glanced back to see Lucian shoot golden fireballs at the angels before he turned and followed them into the jungle.

"Wait!" Lucian gasped. "Stop for a minute."

After running for what seemed like miles through the thick jungle, Dora was relieved to slow down and rest against a tree, brushing the bright green fronds out of her way. The jungle was dark barring the odd ray of bright sunshine that shone through the trees.

It was impossible for the Angel Guard to fly over them here, but that didn't mean they weren't following them on foot.

She glanced in the direction they'd run from, surprised to see that it appeared untouched. There wasn't even a broken branch in their wake.

How is that even possible when we've been running through here like a stampede of elephants?

"What the hell?" She poked a branch that she was

certain she'd just broken as she ran past it. It shimmered with golden light.

"I was just covering our tracks." Lucian shrugged.

"Why is your magic golden?" Dora asked. On earth, and when he was being an asshole, Lucian's magic was a swirling purple cloud. The other angels all shot white magic at people, usually in the form of holy fire. But every time Lucian did something good, it was golden.

He shrugged again.

"The color is a sign of your magical status. Like Kieron's mother is scary fucking green, and I'm er..." Pooey summoned a brown ball of energy in his hands. "Still in deep shit," he muttered.

"Dude, you need to sort that shit out," Lucian stared at the ball of brown energy. "How long has it been like that?"

"A long time," Pooey muttered. "How the fuck did you get golden? No one gets golden energy."

Lucian averted his eyes. "We don't have time for this now. We need to get to the Emerald Garden. Come on. It's this way." He turned and brushed aside a curtain of thick vines, leading them onto a rough trail.

"There's something off about that guy," Pooey muttered.

"Yeah, he's hiding something." Dora nodded as she walked beside him, following Lucian through the jungle.

"Maybe I can get him to tell the truth," Kieron said.

"I dunno. He lies a lot. What does golden mean in terms of magic?" Dora turned to Pooey.

"It's the best. It's the ultimate magic, the most powerful." Pooey muttered.

"How do you know?" Kieron asked before he summoned a silver ball of light. "Silver looks prettier."

"I know because I used to have golden magic before I fucked it all up. It's rare."

Dora stared at Lucian's back as he hurried through the trees ahead. "If he's got ultimate magic, why is he running from the Angel Guard? He can just blast them all can't he?"

"Yeah, and I don't know, but something's off about that guy." Pooey narrowed his eyes at him.

"Nothing about Heaven makes any sense." Dora shrugged. Her idea of Heaven had been completely blown apart by the experience of being in it.

"I know right, where the fuck are all the dead people for starters?" Pooey asked.

Kieron shivered. "Eww, you want to see dead people."

Pooey stared at him in silence for a moment. "What the fuck do you think the ghouls were in Hell, fairies?"

Kieron frowned for a moment. "Yeah, but they weren't icky corpses."

"They were kinda icky," Dora said, remembering Larry, who could fart fire.

Pooey sighed. "Yeah, but where are they in Heaven? I haven't seen one soul since I've been here. Where do all the dead people go?"

Dora frowned. He was right. In Hell, the souls had been everywhere. Souls had been a sick kind of currency. But here in Heaven, there were no souls. "Doesn't anyone get into Heaven anymore? No, wait. I saw some. When I got here, there were lines of people in a waiting room."

"That's limbo," Pooey said. "So they're going to limbo, and then what? Where do they go next? Because the only things in Heaven are fucking angels."

"And monsters," Dora muttered.

Kieron raised an eyebrow. "Monsters?"

"I saw some cannibal angels outside Camp Angel. They tried to eat me." Dora shrugged.

Kieron widened his eyes in horror. "What the fuck?"

She shrugged. "I just thought it was normal for fucked up Heaven."

"Yeah, that's not normal." Pooey shook his head. "I don't know much about this place, but eating people is never fucking normal."

"So there is something really wrong with this place," Dora said.

"More than one thing," Pooey muttered.

SNAKEBITE

Kieron came to a halt, staring ahead at his father. He frowned as he watched Lucian kneeling on all fours ahead. He appeared to be digging a hole in the forest floor with his hands, frantically searching for something.

"What the fuck? Did he fall over again?" Pooey asked, clearly referring to the fact that back on Earth, Lucian had fallen over all the time because he hadn't been used to the Earth's axis.

Kieron glanced back over his shoulder at the little bear, and he offered him a shrug.

Dora came up behind them, frowning at Lucian.

Kieron turned to face the fallen angel who was now ripping his way through the nearby shrubbery, pulling away vines and ferns and muttering to himself. "Maybe he finally lost his marbles."

After watching him in silence for a moment, Pooey stepped forward. "Hey, did you drop your last marble or something?"

Lucian's shoulders dropped as he sighed. Then he peered back over his shoulder with angry eyes. "Don't just stand there. Help me look."

Dora stepped forward. "What are we looking for?"

"The key, it's gotta be here. I know I left it here," he muttered before he resumed pulling apart the undergrowth.

Dora glanced back at Kieron, and judging by her expression, she too thought Lucian had lost his final marble.

"What does this key look like, and what does it open?" Kieron asked, stepping forward.

"Don't stand there, you fool!" Lucian cried.

Kieron jumped back. "Why, what?" He peered down at the muddy earth.

"I haven't searched there yet," Lucian muttered.

Kieron narrowed his eyes and folded his arms.

"Maybe it's mad angel disease." Pooey nudged the ground with his toe, causing Lucian to scramble over and start pulling away golden and green leaves and fronds.

"This is ridiculous. Lucian, what the fuck are you looking for?" Dora asked.

"The key! Are you all stupid? We need the key now. They're coming! Can't you hear it?" Lucian looked up with mud clawed in his hands and streaked across his shirt. His eyes glowed red for an instant before they faded back to brown.

Dora jumped back with a gasp.

On instinct, Kieron jumped between her and Lucian. There was something wrong with him. He studied his father, who was back to clawing the ground again. His shirt sleeves were rolled up with long streaks of mud and dirt down them. Kieron zeroed in on the red rash on his arms. "What the fuck is that?"

He pointed to red veins standing up on his father's arms. Then he gripped his hair, pulling his head up to face him.

A tree of red lines were climbing up his neck and growing across his jawline. He pushed the angel onto his back and ripped open his shirt, to reveal a muscled chest with a rash of red glowing veins on it. "Is he infected?"

Pooey peered down at him with narrowed eyes. "Yeah, but not by anything natural. That's magical."

"How do we cure it?" Kieron stared at his father, who had already scrambled back to his knees and was searching the soil for his imaginary key again.

"We need to find the source." Pooey nodded at Lucian. "It'll probably be on his body."

"I'm not searching his..." Kieron widened his eyes. "There has to be another way."

Pooey's eyes remained narrowed. "There is one."

Dora looked hopefully at the little demon.

Pooey's hand shot out through a throng of vines with lightning speed, gripping something that was hidden behind the bushy ferns of the jungle. Whatever it was, it struggled in his grip as he dragged it out of hiding. "We find the little bitch that did it to him," Pooey ground out as he dragged a long colorful snake out of the undergrowth.

Dora widened her eyes in horror, and she stepped back at the sight of the snake.

Unconcerned by the fact he held a hissing serpent in his hands, Pooey stared at the reptile. "What did you do to my—" He glanced at Lucian. "…weak-minded minion."

The snake bared its fangs, hissing and wriggling in his grip.

"Cut the crap. I know you can fucking talk." Pooey shook it until its teeth rattled.

Kieron sidestepped the writhing snake and stood beside Dora. "Maybe they're both infected," he muttered to her out of the side of his mouth.

She nodded, her eyes never leaving the snake.

"Speak, you slimy bitch." Pooey shook the snake again.

"Pooey, I don't think it can talk," Dora said hesitantly.

"Oh yeah, it's just an innocent snake in the jungle, who just happens to wear the curse of the ancients on its skin." Pooey nodded at the intricate red design on its long green body as he squeezed its throat. "Oh well, I guess I'll just have to kill it then." He extended a single claw across the throat of the creature.

The snake widened its eyes. "Let's not rush into things here," it cried, emitting a small whimper.

Dora's mouth dropped open as she stared at the snake.

Kieron froze, staring at the talking snake in shock. For a serpent, it had a sweet voice. It sounded like a little girl with a slight lisp.

"Oh, now you fucking talk. That's just wonderful. What did you do to him?" Pooey nodded to Lucian, who was still frantically searching the ground.

"I was guarding my home. He threatened it." The snake lowered its head.

"I didn't ask you why you attacked. I ask you what you did." Pooey's voice was dark.

"You're not like most angels." The snake wrapped its tail around his arm, undulating around it.

Pooey smiled nastily at it. "I'm not an angel. That's why I know what you are." He shook its tail off.

"W-what are you?" The snake sounded scared.

Pooey leaned closer. "I'm an ancient demon, just like you, Elyssa." His voice was a deadly whisper.

She widened her eyes. "No, you're dead. You were…" She trailed off as Pooey's eyes glowed with anger.

"Betrayed?" Another claw popped out and pressed against her throat.

"You two know each other?" Kieron asked, eyeing the little demon in a new light. Pooey had never spoken much about his past.

The snake hung her head. "Fuck."

"What did you do to Lucian?" Pooey asked.

"I didn't know he was your friend." She shook her head.

"He isn't." Pooey shrugged. "But you're going to restore him all the same."

"I've turned over a new leaf. I-I'm not the same—" The snake began.

"My inner violin is playing for you. Break the spell!" Pooey shook her again. He paused when he noticed that Lucian was stuffing leaves into his mouth and eating them. There was an obvious moment of indecision as Pooey smirked at seeing Lucian chewing dirt and leaves.

"Pooey," Kieron warned. "He's still my father."

The little bear rolled his eyes. "Fix him."

"I can't work miracles. I'll remove the spell, but the rest of him is your problem," the snake muttered as she glowed. She closed her eyes and her form shimmered, transforming from a snake into a young woman. She was only small, about four feet tall, even shorter now since she was kneeling in Pooey's grasp. Her golden hair flowed down her back in waves meeting the pale silk of her dress. She looked like a little angel without wings.

She held out her hands and aimed them at Lucian. A pale blue light shone in her eyes as she cast a cloud of blue smoke at the fallen angel. It surrounded him before evaporating into his skin.

Kieron watched as the red veins in his father's skin faded away and comprehension grew in his eyes as he chewed on a leaf.

Lucian widened his eyes. Then he spat out the leaves in his mouth, choking for a moment. "What the fuck is this shit?" He spat out the foliage.

Pooey smirked, his claws still around the girl's throat. "You're welcome."

The girl turned to Pooey, reaching out to touch his face.

He jerked his head out of her way.

"What happened to you?" She sounded awestruck.

He narrowed his eyes. "Is the snake bit karma?" he asked, ignoring her question.

"I was going for irony." She shrugged. "Garden of Eden and all that."

"I thought the Garden of Eden was on Earth." Dora frowned.

"That was the last version of it. This is the beta." The girl nodded back to the vines that Pooey had pulled her out of. "They called it the Emerald Garden."

Lucian looked up. "Is anyone going to tell me why

the fuck I was eating leaves?"

"My ex gave you magical herpes," Pooey muttered.

"It was just a bite!" Elyssa said.

"Why did you bite him?" Kieron asked.

She batted her blue eyes at Kieron. "I was just protecting my home."

"Your home is the Emerald Garden, but I thought you were from Hell?" Dora asked skeptically.

"What makes you think I'm from Hell?" Elyssa asked, staring at her with wide, innocent blue eyes.

"Oh hello, did you forget me in Hell again?" Pooey pushed her away from him. Then he muttered a spell under his breath.

Silver chains appeared around her wrists. She widened her eyes. Then she scowled at Pooey. "You wouldn't dare…"

"See what I did. I fucking dared. Aren't you going to invite us into your home?"

She narrowed her eyes at Pooey. "You're a monster. Where is the kind man I once knew?"

Pooey pushed her towards the vines. "You made him into a demon," he muttered as he pushed her through the vines. "Take us to the Emerald Garden."

SECRET IDENTITY

Dora scowled at the back of their new companion, Elyssa. She kept shooting innocent looks at Kieron, who seemed sympathetic to her.

Dora didn't know about Pooey's history, but she trusted the little demon with her life. She'd never seen him so angry before. This was the creature that had sent him to Hell. It had turned Lucian into a dribbling idiot with just one bite, and now her serpent eyes were settled on Kieron.

Clenching her jaw, Dora tried to think rationally, but it was impossible when it came to Kieron. She'd only just got him back. Nothing was going to separate them again, and this new encounter seemed like a threat to her.

Oh great, I'm turning into a jealous girlfriend.

She tried to shake off the feeling. It was irrational jealousy, wasn't it?

She caught Elyssa watching her with a nasty smile before it was quickly replaced by an innocent expression.

Then again…

"We need to ditch the fucking snake," Lucian muttered as he sidled up to Dora, matching her pace.

For once, Dora agreed with the fallen angel. Elyssa was a threat. She could feel it.

"Pooey seems to have her under control." She tried to be fair to the girl.

"She's his ex. He's never had her under control."

Dora frowned at Lucian. What was that supposed to mean?

"Love blinds everyone, even your little ninja." Lucian sighed.

"Pooey's not in love." Dora shook her head.

"He was once, and it doesn't go away." Lucian stared across the rolling green fields of the Emerald Garden. "Love never ends. It never lets you go."

For a moment, she wondered which love he was speaking of. Then her eyes fell upon Kieron. She couldn't imagine a world without him. It was true. Love wound around your heart until it became a part of you. It felt as if she would lose a part of her if she ever lost Kieron. She'd always love him, no matter what happened.

"So Pooey's still under her spell," Dora muttered.

"Yeah, and take it from someone who's been under one of her spells, it's not a fucking nice place to be."

"What is she, a demon?" Dora asked.

Lucian shook his head. "I don't know. She shouldn't be here."

"But there was a snake in the Garden of Eden. At least, that's what the bible said."

Lucian rolled his eyes. "Yeah, and according to that patriarchal bullshit, Eve was made from a rib of Adam, except that would impossible since all life begins as female. If you believe the bible, we have more problems than a couple of demons."

"What is the bible? I mean really, what was it?"

Lucian shook his head. "It was entertainment. It was God's fucking comic book. Some of the authors were awesome, and some of them sucked. It was a narrative, just another narrative."

Dora frowned. "But people believe in it. People die for it! You can't just…" She shook her head. "It has to mean something."

"It does to the people who believe that story. All of this, reality and the world, it grows from a narrative. The stories define who we are. They define the world. Angels believe in God because of the stories about him. He isn't even here anymore, but they make him real because they believe his stories. Faith in stories is our greatest strength and our greatest weakness."

She turned to face him. "That's oddly profound for you. What do you believe in?"

"I believe in the power of stories." He winked. "But I don't believe the stories."

"What does that make you?" she asked.

"A writer," he muttered.

"So what are angels then, writers?"

"Oh no, they're just messengers. They just deliver the stories."

"No, they save people, don't they?"

Lucian rolled his eyes. "You don't even know the narrative of your own world. No wonder you don't understand Heaven. The word angel means messenger. That's it."

"Like the postman?" Dora frowned.

"Yeah, angels are the celestial postmen."

"So this is just the sorting office?" Dora asked, skeptical about Lucian's answers. She was itching to Google the word 'angel'.

The corners of his mouth curved up into a smile. "Now, you're getting it. Do you see any dead souls here, living out their final days surrounded by warmth and happiness? Are these the Elysian Fields?" He gestured to the endless garden.

"Well, no, but I saw people when I first got here." Dora nodded.

"And where are they now?"

Dora frowned. "I don't know. What happened to them?"

He shrugged. "Redistribution, recycling, logistical relocation…"

"Reincarnation?" she asked.

"Sometimes. Other times they become mulch and go back into the Earth. That life goes into a tree that watches over earth like a sentinel for thousands of years, giving air to the other living things around it. We never die. We are remolded into new life over and over again in different forms. There is no end for anyone. There is no eternal torment, and there is no happy ever after. Live your life well because if you fuck up, you can't lose it even if you want to. The only thing that can destroy us is ourselves."

"But what about Hell? I've been there. I know it exists." Dora shook her head.

"Was it Hell, really, or was it just another narrative?"

She thought about it. It wasn't that bad for Hell, not really. "There is no such thing as Heaven or Hell!" She widened her eyes. "Where the fuck are we then?"

"It's just another plain of existence, one where they believe in Heaven. But there are only angels here besides us."

"Because they believe in it, it's created by what they believe in."

He nodded.

She narrowed her eyes at him. "So God is just the author of it."

"What?" He widened his eyes in innocence. "No, I dunno…" He looked away.

"Someone had to create the idea of Heaven, and you said you were a writer."

"Your idea of Heaven was created on Earth as a threat. Does this sound familiar: *You won't get into Heaven if you don't do as I say?*" Lucian shook his head. "The concept of Heaven was created to control people. The reality of it would be insane. Imagine your perfect Heaven. Then imagine it every day for eternity. Is it still perfect?"

Lucian frowned into the distance. "The only thing that can be constant is change. The same thing every day, no matter what it is, is dull monotony. If there's one thing I've learned, it's that you can't create a perfect existence."

"But you tried to, didn't you?" Dora studied him, a shocking realization forming in her mind. He knew too much for it not to be true, but he refused to look her in the eye.

"Oh look, the Grotto." He pointed to a massive castle in the distance. "We're nearly home." He rushed off, leaving her staring after him in shock.

No, he can't be. He's too much of an asshole.

She shook her head, trying to ignore the sinking feeling that she'd just discovered Lucian's secret.

THE NAME OF GOD

D ora caught up with Kieron as they entered the
gates to the old castle, a broken old building
that had clearly once been grand. The spires
shone with golden tiles on the roof, and the walls were
smooth like glass, but they were cracked and worn
away by time.

She turned her eyes to Kieron, drinking in his
golden hair and bright blue eyes. If her suspicions were
correct, she was dating the son of… She shook her
head.

*I must be wrong. It makes no sense. None of this
makes any sense.*

She curled her fingers around Kieron's hand,
holding onto the only thing in her world that still did
make sense.

He squeezed her hand and smiled at her. When he

saw her expression, he frowned. "Are you okay, Dora-minx?"

"What do you think God is like?" she asked.

He thought about it for a moment. "He's probably an over-powered dick, who doesn't care about anyone."

She glanced at Lucian.

From the mouths of babes...

She tried to think about their situation, about their mission as they walked towards the open door of the castle. The darkness inside it seemed haunted by ghosts of the past.

What am I worrying about? My father was right. God's been watching over me all along.

She felt a wry smile grow on her face. Her father would renounce his faith if he believed that Lucian was God. Her father had his own narrative, and even though he'd opened up to the more peaceful side of faith—forgiveness and love—he'd still flip his shit if this reality shattered his delusions.

Maybe delusions are what keep us from going insane?

She frowned as they stepped through the doorway into a dark and broken palace.

Look what happened to John Lennon when he asked people to imagine there was no Heaven. They shot him for it. People like to be delusional. That's why lies are always easier to believe.

Dora felt a shock of revelation as she stared around the broken foyer.

Is my faith untrue? Is magic a lie too?

She tried to shake herself out of it, but there were too many questions. Now that her delusions had been shattered, she was questioning everything, and it was driving her a bit insane. Life had never been easy, but it had been clear. She'd always known who she was and what she wanted. Now, in the face of an altered reality, she wasn't even certain that Kieron's warm hand gripping hers was real, and she needed that to be real.

"This is a grotto?" Pooey stepped into the room behind them, and his voice echoed around the large atrium. "It's a bit opulent isn't it?"

"It's the house of God, you idiot," Elyssa muttered beside him.

"It's not a fucking grotto. It's a dilapidated Disney palace." Pooey ground out the words.

"We won't be safe here for long. So let's get what we came for and get the hell out of this place."

Dora jumped at the sound of Lucian's voice. She glanced at him. He was still playing the role of the fallen angel, but she knew better now. She wondered why he was hiding at all. If he was God, surely he could control the armies of Heaven. Was this all just a game to him?

She frowned.

Maybe I'm wrong. Maybe Elyssa's venom drove me nuts too.

It was a possibility. It made more sense than Lucian being God. Deciding to find out one way or the other, she galvanized herself into action.

"Let's stop wasting time and find God then shall we?" She released Kieron's hand and stepped towards the open doorway ahead. "Search the place. There has to be an answer here somewhere."

Dora stared around the empty bedroom, averting her eyes from the dusty harp near the window. The room was familiar, and not in a good way. It was scarily similar to Lucian's room in his other palace. She'd been trying to pretend that it was all a mistake, but the more she delved through God's belongings, the more they seemed like Lucian's.

She shook her head and pulled open the closet. It was filled with shirts, old ones that were pocked with holes by moths now.

"This is just weird."

Kieron's voice behind her made her jump.

"Which part?" she asked.

"Everything about this place is weird. I can't..." He paused for a moment, shaking his head. "Maybe it's just an angel thing."

Dora turned to face him, curious about what he meant. If Kieron noticed the same thing she had, then it would be proof that she hadn't gone insane. "What's an angel thing?"

"Well, this place, I can't help but feel that…" He paused again.

"Yes?"

"It's really crazy."

"That's okay. What is it?"

"It's Lucian's. I know it's crazy, but even these shirts look like his." Kieron plucked the arm of one of the shirts, shaking his head. "Maybe I'm going crazy." He sighed.

"You're not the only one."

"I think Lucian might be—" Kieron began.

"God." Dora finished for him.

"What?" He widened his eyes. "I was going to say lying to us."

"Oh, right. Yeah, that's possible too, I guess." She winced.

"What do you mean? Do you think he's God?"

She frowned. "He said that the world was just a lot of stories, angels were just messengers and that he was a writer. If the world is just created from stories, and he's the writer, then…" She trailed off, realizing that she sounded crazy. It made more sense when he'd said it.

"No, he can't be. I-I…That would make me…" Kieron widened his eyes in horror. "Oh, fuck that!"

"I might be wrong." She shrugged.

"But this is his house." Kieron scowled at the

shirts. "This is his fucking house. I can feel it. Come on." He gripped her hand and pulled her towards the door.

"Where are we going?"

"We're going to find out once and for all."

"How?"

"We're going to ask him."

"Ask who, what?" Pooey asked as they entered the hallway.

"We're going to interrogate Lucian," Kieron said.

Dora noticed the muscles in his jaw clench as if he was holding in the rest of the sentence.

"Oh, count me in. Maybe Elyssa can make him eat leaves again." Pooey grinned.

"Now, you want my help." Elyssa folded her arms and narrowed her eyes.

How did she even touch Lucian if he is God?

Dora eyed Elyssa with suspicion. There were a lot of questions that she needed answering. She nodded. "Let's go find him."

They found Lucian in the kitchen. He was about to take a bite out of a giant cheeseburger. He paused with his mouth open over the elaborate creation. Then he closed his mouth and sighed as he put the burger down. "What now?"

"Interrogation time, bitch." Pooey took a seat beside him at the counter, and he eyed the burger. "Is that pickle relish?"

"Yeah, are we good now? Is the interrogation over?" Lucian reclined in his chair and stared at Dora and Kieron.

Kieron stepped forward. "Are you…" He paused, shooting a glance at Dora.

She nodded. They had to ask, no matter how stupid it sounded. "Are you God?" she asked.

"What?" Pooey cried before he started laughing. He turned to Lucian, wiping tears from his eyes. "Yeah, Fallen Fail, are you the almighty, or has everyone been drinking the elixir of insanity?"

Lucian remained silent for a moment. Then he picked up his cheeseburger and took a bite before slowly chewing it and swallowing. The room fell deadly silent as they all stared at each other.

"Seriously?" Pooey widened his eyes before he jumped off the seat beside Lucian and took a step back.

Lucian sighed. "Yeah, so what?" He shrugged before taking another bite from his burger.

"But you left Heaven. You can't be Him!" Elyssa stepped away from Lucian as far as her chains would allow.

Lucian frowned at her.

She looked around panicked and then seemed to gather her wits before shouting: "You abandoned us!"

"I didn't abandon you. *You* weren't even supposed to be here." Lucian narrowed his eyes at her. "You're no angel, no matter how much cute little girl you slap onto your face."

Elyssa widened her eyes in horror. "You know what I am?"

"Do you?" he asked.

She frowned. "I-I don't understand. I did penance. I—"

He widened his eyes. "Oh that's what it is. I don't know why I didn't notice before." He stood up, walking towards her.

"No, stay back." She held up her hands as if to ward him off.

He clenched his jaw and reached out to touch her face. Then he scowled. "You're not a demon or an angel."

Pooey frowned at Elyssa. "What is she then?"

Elyssa dodged out of Lucian's grasp and rushed to the windows, clearly planning to jump out of one.

Lucian waved his hand, and the windows and doors in the room all disappeared.

"What is she?" Dora asked, frowning as she stared at the wall where the window had just been.

Elyssa turned around and glared at Lucian. "You think you're so powerful, as if you're the only one who can have any fun." Her eyes glowed red as she turned to face him, and her cherubic face pinched into a pure evil scowl.

Kieron backed away from her. "What the fuck is she?"

"She's a fucking writer!" Lucian stepped towards her.

"What, like you are?" Dora asked.

Pooey tilted his head to the side. "Does that make her into God too?"

"No, it fucking doesn't!" Lucian flashed him a look of anger. "It makes her the creature that brought the brainwashing here." He turned to her. "It was you, wasn't it? You're the corporation."

She shook her head at him. "I'm just a tiny cog in a greater design. You think you're the only one who can create, but you're not!" She spat at him.

"You only destroyed things!" He shouted at her.

She laughed bitterly. "It didn't work anyway. I didn't get my happy ending, but it was worth it just to mess with you."

Lucian rubbed his eyes, expelling a frustrated sigh. "Fucking idiots, I'm surrounded by fucking idiots," he muttered.

"Hey!" Kieron and Dora shouted in unison.

Pooey just stared at Elyssa.

"Not you this time." Lucian waved them away before turning back to Elyssa. "A happy ending, is that why you did it?" His dark eyes shone with a light of sarcasm.

"Why not? I deserve one!" Elyssa cried.

"Oh yeah, I can see that. Brainwashed angels, cannibals, fracking, the Republicans, even Hell can't

199

contain that much evil!"

"I didn't create the Republicans," Elyssa widened her eyes in innocence. "They were someone else's evil creation!"

"So you were the one who stopped the angels from using their wings, who brainwashed or threatened them into following your orders, and for what?" Lucian shook his head at her.

"My happy fucking ending," she cried. "But I didn't get it, did I? So it was all for nothing."

"Can you give Lettuce his mind back?" Pooey asked, frowning at his ex.

She shrugged. "It wasn't much of a brain to begin with, but yeah."

Lucian held up his hand to silence Pooey before turning back to Elyssa. "Do you know why you didn't get your happy ending?"

"Yes! They took it. They took over. Fluffers and his fucking Angel Guard took it before they locked me up in here as some kind of fucking deity. They took my happy ending!"

"Wrong," Lucian said in a quiet voice. "There is no such fucking thing as a happy ending!" he shouted. "You fucking idiot! You get one existence, one!" He held up his finger to illustrate his point. "What you do with that existence will dictate your future. No one took shit from you. You had everything you needed to build what you wanted. All you had to do was make the right choices, and that little feeling in your gut is your guide. You *know* when you do something wrong. Seriously, I gave you all an internal warning system, your conscience! Is it that difficult to follow it?" He shook his head. "If you want a happy ending, to have everything in this world and the next, then you have to fucking earn it!"

"Bullshit, everyone has more than me, even that pathetic fucking demon." She pointed to Pooey.

He pointed to Pooey. "Even the wicked fucking demons know the difference between right and wrong, but not you."

Pooey beamed. "He thinks I'm badass, and fuck you, Elyssa."

Lucian laughed. "Do you think that everyone is blessed but you? Do you think that no one else suffers? Are you really so small-minded that you think some people are handed everything on a plate?"

"Well, yeah."

"Just because they don't bitch and complain about it, it doesn't mean they haven't been through hell. Anyone who is sitting on top of the world had to move mountains to get there. Anyone who still isn't happy when they get there, hurt someone to get what they wanted. The happiest beings in existence don't take anything from anyone. They give to the universe instead!"

"Oh that self-sacrifice bullshit, yeah that worked

out well for all your martyrs. What about royalty? They just inherit their stuff. Do you want to know what my happy ending will be?" She snarled at Lucian. "It'll be watching all your angels become braindead, watching the corporation burn you all up, not because it's all-powerful, but because you let it! Then I'll be fucking happy."

"Have you ever seen a happy member of royalty? No, me either. Wealth isn't happiness. It's just another punishment."

"Oh yeah, being the most powerful is useless." She shook her head. "You're fucking insane."

"True power comes from freedom, and wealth doesn't give you that. Nothing can give you that because you're born with it inside you. Freedom is something you are born with. It's up to you if you let someone take it away from you. Fight for your freedom or live in a cage. The most powerful people in the world are the ones that are free of all the cages around them, including wealth!"

"True power comes from this palace." Elyssa shot a sly smile at him.

"Where is it?" Lucian shot her a bored look.

"Where is what?" She widened her eyes in an innocent expression.

"You know what." He held up his hand and summoned a purple ball of energy in it. "You didn't do all this with your scrappy powers."

"I'll die before I tell you!" she screamed.

"That can be arranged. You can die, and then you'll tell me," he said in a quiet, deadly tone.

"Fine, then do it!" she snapped.

Lucian stepped closer to Elyssa, his knuckles whitening around the ball of energy.

Dora panicked. She didn't want anyone to die. "No don't!" She stepped forward and gripped his arm.

He turned his head to face her with lightning speed. His eyes glowed golden with a fire in them that caused her to stumble back. She shook her head, ignoring the spike of fear that shot down her spine. "This isn't who you are."

"What makes you think that you know who I am?" He glared at her.

"Because I never fell for your bullshit. I never had blind faith." She didn't know why she said that to an almighty pissed off being, but it was Lucian. She knew this wasn't who he really was. Lucian's revenge was an elastic band whapping you in the face for all eternity, not a final, fiery death.

He stared at her in silence for a moment. Then he extinguished the ball of energy with a shake of his head. "You're my fucking conscience, my curse," he said to Dora. "Of all the cosmic jokes, how did I end up with *you* as my Jiminy fucking Cricket?"

"Just lucky I guess." She shrugged.

"You're all so... so fucking pathetic." Elyssa shook

her head. "The corporation told me to watch out for you. Fluffers told me that my greatest challenge would be Dora and her band of misfits. You even have God on your side, and you're useless." She expelled a crazy laugh. "You can't even kill one angel!"

"Fucking an angel doesn't make you into one." Lucian said.

"Thank fuck for that," Kieron muttered.

Lucian stared at him. "That just means that your mother isn't one. You still are." Then he waved his hand at Elyssa, and she disappeared, evaporating out of the room.

"Shit." Kieron sighed and shook his head.

25

THE ALMIGHTY ALARM

"What did you do to her?" Pooey cried, running over to the spot where she had been standing.

"I sent her to the place of happy endings. It's full of psychopaths, sociopaths and evil masterminds. They all wanted a happy ever after, so I gave them exactly what they asked for." Lucian displayed a smile that caused a shiver to shoot down Dora's spine. She didn't know where he'd sent Elyssa, but she was certain it wasn't a happy place.

"Dude, you have the worst taste in women." Lucian shook his head.

"You can't just—" Pooey began.

"Yeah, I can. She broke my Heaven. I can kick her ass out of it."

"If you're God, why did you leave Heaven? Why

is it so fucked up here? Why is the world so fuc—"
Dora didn't get to finish as Lucian held up his hand,
silencing her.

"Hold on there. Once you go down that path, the
questions never end, and your answer is just that. The
questions never ended!" Lucian turned to face her.
"Being creative is the worst curse, you know. I was just
floating in the ether. I was happy. I could have stayed
that way. But nooooo, I decided that I was going to
create something beautiful. That's when it always goes
wrong, you know."

He paced the room, his expression serious. He
turned to face Dora, Kieron and Pooey. "Do you want
to know why I left? Stupid fucking questions, that's
why. I created the world. I created everything, Heaven,
Hell, angels and demons. I created people, the Earth,
multitudes of complex ecosystems and lifeforms, and
what did I get in return? Did anyone thank me? No!
They fucking complained. Why does the washing
machine steal a sock? Shouldn't my ass be smaller? Why
can't I have more? On and on, my artwork became the
land of fucking customer support, and I wasn't even
selling anything!"

"Even now, when I'm gone for thousands of years,
these motherfuckers complain. Do you know how un-
fucking-sexy it is to hear your name cried out every
time someone fakes an orgasm?"

"So you just left?" Dora frowned at him.

"Hell yes, I left. I fucked it all off. I just created the place. A call center in India can deal with the customer support for all I fucking care! Enjoy the universe or don't. I don't give a shit. It's free art, enjoy it while it lasts!"

"What do you mean, *while it lasts*?" Dora widened her eyes.

"Well, the latest narrative of capitalism is going to fuck it all up. People are being drugged by false narratives while the world is being destroyed around them. It probably won't end well." Lucian shrugged. "Still, if you sit in your fucking armchair watching *The Briefcase* while someone fracks under your house, and the house falls on top of you, you only have yourself to blame."

"Why don't you do something about all the death and destruction then?" Dora cried. "You have the power to fix everything. Aren't you just sitting in your fucking armchair, watching *The Briefcase*?"

"Don't be ridiculous. *Supernatural* is much more my style," Lucian muttered.

Dora raised an eyebrow.

"I don't know how many times I have to tell you that I don't give a fuck for it to sink in, but I really don't give a fuck anymore. My days of trying to fix this shit are over. Do you want to know what helping gets you? It gets you more fucking complaints. They complained it was too hot, so I gave them an Ice Age, and they're still fucking bitching about it!"

Kieron nodded. "They still complain about that in Hell too."

"So, what, you're just going to go back to Earth to get drunk until the world ends?" Dora asked. "That's the grand plan?"

"Hey, I just created it. I'm not responsible for everyone in the universe."

"Yes, you are!" Dora was about to flip her shit. She didn't believe in much, but God was supposed to care. Even in her agnostic world, God was supposed to care about something.

"Why?" He frowned. "I created independent lifeforms. They can take care of themselves and each other. Why should I try when they don't?"

"Why didn't you make them want to try more?" Pooey asked. "Like, why not create a God's call center and have like really annoying self-righteous music playing on it while they're on hold? Why not make everyone give more of a shit?"

"Free will," Lucian muttered. "I hard-coded them with free will. I can't make them do shit they don't want to, not really. Plus, I'm pretty sure working in God's call center would be worse than Hell. That'd just be cruel."

Pooey nodded. "It would make an awesome punishment in Hell."

"This is ridiculous." Dora turned on her heel. "Just

get us the fuck out of here. You can do that, can't you?" She glanced over her shoulder at Lucian. She couldn't understand her disappointment. She'd never really believed in God anyway, but she'd been oddly looking forward to meeting him. Now that she had, she wasn't sure she'd ever believe in anything again. The world really was fucked, and she wanted to make it better.

Apparently, it won't be getting any better because God can't be assed to fix it!

She spun around and scowled at him.

"What about the fucking Angel Guard. Don't you control them?"

Kieron widened his eyes. "Why didn't you stop the Angel Guard? All this time, you could have just commanded them to stop!"

"Fuck that. All this time, you could have clicked your fingers and brought Dora back to life. We didn't even have to come here! What kind of god are you?" Pooey cried.

Lucian narrowed his eyes. Then he expelled a long, drawn-out sigh. "Do you honestly think I came back here by choice?"

"Why not? Your palace is here, oh mighty one." Pooey scowled at him and folded his arms.

"Why didn't use your powers to avoid coming here?" Dora asked, her interest piqued.

"Yeah, why go through all this bullshit?" Kieron added.

"Because I didn't have my fucking powers!" Lucian shouted, his face turning red with anger and embarrassment. "That bitch stole them. How do you think she fucked up Heaven?"

"Huh?" Pooey frowned at him, but his next question was cut off as a loud alarm blared through the palace.

Dora jumped at the sound of the alarm, which gave off a high-pitched squeal that sent shock waves through her and caused a bubble of panic to swell in the back of her throat. "What the hell is that noise?" she shouted over the din.

"Shit, it's the Almighty Alarm."

"What the fuck is that?" Pooey cried before covering his ears with his hands.

"It means that God has returned. They know I'm here," Lucian muttered.

GENESIS

L ucian waved his hand, and a window appeared in the wall where it had once been.

Dora stared out of the window, and she swallowed a bubble of panic as she watched thousands of angels landing on the lawn outside. The garden rapidly filled with the Angel Guard, the villagers and thousands of other angels. Even the cannibals were outside, snapping at nearby angels.

Her heart jumped in her chest when she saw Lillian thrown to her knees in front of the grotto by a massive member of the Angel Guard. The young angel still looked as if she had her mind, and there was fear in her big blue eyes as she looked at the palace, as if fearing the punishment that was to come.

But then, that's what Heaven has been used as all this time hasn't it, some kind of control device.

Lettuce landed on the lawn, staring blankly at the window as if he didn't know why he was here.

"What are they going to do?" she asked.

The angels charged at the palace with a roar, some wielding weapons. The walls shook as they banged against them with their fists, screaming out for their God.

"Worship me to death," Lucian muttered before he waved his hand, and the window disappeared again.

The palace shook from the riot outside it.

"What are we going to do?" Kieron stared at Lucian in horror. "Can't you stop them?"

He scowled. "Not without my powers. And I don't want them. I don't want to be God anymore."

"Clearly, you still are whether you want to be or not," Dora said, pointing to the shaking wall as cracks began to appear in it.

He scowled. "I forgot about the stupid fucking alarm."

"Well, thanks for that epiphany. Now, how do we get the fuck out of here?" Pooey asked.

Lucian frowned. "We can't, not without my powers." He studied Dora for a moment in silence. Then he sighed. "We need to find them."

"I thought Elyssa stole them," Kieron said.

"She did, but they can't leave this place. They're rooted here. We need to find them before the angels get in here." Lucian jumped back as a large piece of masonry fell from the cracked ceiling and smashed into the spot he'd been standing in.

Dora peered up. The roof was cracking under the pressure of thousands of angels stampeding on it. "We better hurry before they get in here." She flashed a warning look at Lucian. "I guess you're going to have to take responsibility for your creation after all."

"Yeah..." He looked away, shaking his head.

"Where do we start looking?" Pooey cried as another slab of marble smashed into the floor beside him.

"She was your fucking girlfriend! Where would she hide things?" Lucian shouted over the din of the angel riot, which was echoing around the room as more cracks appeared in the walls.

"I don't fucking kno—" Pooey paused. "She liked creepy, dark places! Do you have like a dungeon or something?"

"There are underground tunnels." Lucian nodded. "We'll be safer down there too. Come on!"

He led them out of the kitchen into a crumbling foyer. Wild angel eyes peered through the broken wood in the door as they tried to break through it.

"Why are they fucking squeeing like a troop of teenage girls at a Bieber concert?" Pooey asked.

Lucian ignored the question as he pulled open the door beneath the sweeping staircase. "Stupid questions later," he said as he waved them over.

They hurried down a stone staircase as Lucian closed the door behind them,

Dora glanced back to see him cast a spell over the door, sealing it with a golden light. Then he hurried after them into a dark abyss below.

Lucian clicked his fingers behind them, and the tunnel lit up with burning torches that were attached to the walls. "We'll look in the main hall first." He rushed past her, taking the lead and heading down the long tunnel.

There's a main hall down here?

She hurried after him, glancing unsurely at the walls beside her. Hairline cracks were appearing in them with each shake of the building.

It must be complete chaos upstairs.

"You need to fix everything, Lucian. This shouldn't be happening." She called out after him, hurrying to keep up.

"Yeah, whatever," he muttered.

"You have a responsibility to make everything right," she said. "You know, that little feeling in your gut."

He expelled a laugh as he turned to glance at her over his shoulder. "I don't have a conscience, unless we're considering you for the job."

"But you said…" She trailed off.

"I said that you were my conscience. I don't have one, but I don't seem to be able to get rid of your nagging voice, do I?"

"I know a way you can get rid of it," she said.

He looked hopeful for a moment.

"Do what I tell you to do, and I'll shut up."

He scowled. "Now, that'd be a fucking miracle."

"I'm only trying to help." She frowned at him. "You know I'm right."

He studied her for a moment. "Maybe you can help, but first we need to get my powers."

She nodded as they entered a massive old hall. It was dotted with broken statues and old pillars. Turning around she scanned the room, her eyes drawn to a glowing light at the back of the chamber. "Where would she have hidden it?"

Lucian stared at back of the room, appearing deep in thought as Kieron and Pooey ran through the entrance behind them.

"Hurry!" Kieron gasped, pointing behind him. "They're coming!"

Dora glanced back to see the roof of the tunnel crumbling away outside the hall and thousands of angels clawing their way through the debris.

"What do we do?" she cried at Lucian.

He slowly turned and scanned the chaos ahead of him. Then he snapped out of his contemplation. "I'll hold them back. You need to go and get that golden glowing thing for me."

"I'll get it," Pooey said.

"No, I need you and Kieron to help me fight. Dora's the weakest. She can get it for me." He pointed to her. "Hurry!"

She nodded and then turned on her heel and raced down the hall towards the golden glow. Her pulse raced as she hurried away from the sounds of blasts behind her.

As she drew closer, she realized that the golden glow was coming from an object on top of an altar. It was contained inside a glass case, and it was a quill, a golden quill.

She rushed to the altar, glancing back over her shoulder to see that Lucian had created some kind of magical barrier that was holding back the armies of Heaven.

She turned to look at the quill. It was beautiful with intricate patterns across the golden feathers.

I guess it makes sense for a writer.

Jumping at the loud crash behind her, she spun around to see the ceiling cave in at the center of the hall. Giant stone slabs and broken walls crashed down, revealing a giant hole in the ceiling and blue skies above it. The palace must have been demolished above them.

Hundreds of angels swooped down into the room.

Without waiting to find out what they would do, she punched through the glass case, shattering it, and she grabbed the golden quill in her hand.

The world shifted, and her arm felt as if it had been

electrocuted. She peered down to see it glowing with a golden light.

"Oh shit."

In slow motion, she saw Kieron shouting her name. Angels ran past Lucian and made a beeline for her instead. Then a blast of golden light exploded out of her.

She caught a wry smile appearing on Lucian's face as he turned towards her.

"Lucian, you fucking dick!" she cried as she lit up like a beacon, golden rays coming off her and filling the room in a blast of unbelievable power.

The forces of the universe coursed through her, and she screamed in agony.

Kieron stared in horror as Dora exploded into a ball of golden light. "No!" he cried, running towards her.

Lucian pulled him back, and he turned to glare at him. "What did you do to her?"

"Nothing. She'll be fine." He shrugged. "She wanted to fix the universe, so I let her."

Kieron widened his eyes as he realized what Lucian had done. "No!" He pushed Lucian away from him and ran down the hall towards her.

The light faded from her, and she fell to her knees before the army of angels who were charging at her.

I'll save her. I can save her. I can—

He froze when she looked up, and her eyes glowed with gold. Her form altered before his eyes, transforming into someone else. Dora disappeared and an angry old man with a long white beard stood in the place where Dora had once been.

The angels heading for her came to an unsure halt in front of Him.

God slowly stood up, never taking his fiery eyes off the creatures ahead of Him. Sunlight shone from beneath his skin, and electricity crackled in the air around Him.

Thousands of angels dropped to their knees before the being, bowing their heads in submission to their god.

I AM SPARTACUS

Dora stared ahead at the hall full of angels while her body tingled with a rush of power. She felt as if she could fly. She felt as if she could do anything. It was the weirdest feeling she'd ever experienced. Power pulsed through her veins, and she could see it. In her mind, she could follow her own veins and see all the different cells doing different things. She could feel the fabric of the universe and see how it all worked. It was fucking bizarre.

Distracted by a million new senses, she tried to focus on the room, but everything in it was a living organism with complex threads weaving through them.

Kieron's voice pierced through her daze, and she turned to focus on him, trying to listen to what he was saying, but there were so many voices coming from him.

"What did you do to her, you fucker?" Kieron shouted.

At the same time, a worried Kieron said: *"Is she going to be okay?"*

Shortly afterwards, a sad Kieron said: *"I can't lose her now. She promised not to die on me!"*

She stared at him, trying to work out if he had three voices or not. Then it dawned on her that she was reading his mind. Judging by the way he was gripping Lucian's collar and shouting in his face, she guessed that the first comment had been words. Focusing on that, she tried to filter out his thoughts.

A part of her idly wondered if she should poke around in there, but she sensed that it would lead to more trouble than it was worth. Right now, she needed to get a grip.

She peered at Pooey, trying to focus on something less complicated, and widened her eyes. She could see the little brown werebear, but around him was the genetic frame of a huge beast that looked a bit like a wookie to her. Pooey's internal magic was at least six feet tall.

Curious, she peered into Pooey's mind. There was a locked door in there, which she had to go around. Once she got past it, his thoughts flooded out.

"I want some cheesy puffs."

"I wonder if God can summon me a mountain of cheesy puffs."

"Where's Dora gone"

"Lucian's a fucking dick! I hope God turns him into an amoeba."

"Did God eat Dora?"

He studied her with curious eyes. *"Why's He looking at me like that? Does God eat demons?"* Pooey narrowed his eyes at her.

Frowning, she glanced at Lucian. His eyes glittered as if he knew exactly what she was doing. She pushed against the barriers around his mind, and he pushed back.

Has he been reading our minds all this time?

"No, I fucking haven't." His reply echoed in her thoughts.

"Then how did you know what I was fucking thinking?" She narrowed her eyes at him.

"You put the question in my head." He shrugged.

"Why did you do this to me, you asshole?" she silently asked.

"I'm tired of this shit, and you seem to want to fix the world. Now's your chance." He flashed a wicked grin.

"You're a complete dick. You know that, right?" Breaking the connection, she stared at the armies of Heaven, who were waiting patiently for her to speak.

Okay, screw Lucian and his bullshit. I can do this.

"RELEASE THE ANGEL." She pointed to Lillian. The sound of her voice shocked her. It was hollow and full of power, nothing like her usual voice.

Clearly, it shocked the Angel Guard too, who quickly unchained Lillian and set her free before bowing down to Dora again.

She turned to Kieron, who was staring at her with wide eyes. "THIS WILL BE INTERESTING." She frowned. Her voice sounded wrong, but she couldn't seem to make it go back to normal.

Kieron took a step back, concern furrowing his brow. "Give me back Dora."

"I AM DORA." She took a step towards him, and he backed away again.

Oh for fucksake, what is this?

"Why is God pretending to be Dora, and what the fuck did He do with her?" Pooey asked.

Dora glanced at Lucian, who gave her a shrug. It seemed that Pooey and Kieron saw something else when they saw her now. "NO REALLY, I AM DORA."

Pooey narrowed his eyes. "No, I am Spartacus." Then he widened his eyes. "You don't fry beings for sarcasm do you?"

"Give me Dora back!" Kieron shouted at her, his eyes full of fire.

She smiled at his protective side. She'd never seen it from this angle before. He was fierce when he was fighting for her. "AWW, THAT'S SWEET."

His eyes became slits as he summoned a ball of silver light in his hands. "You're mocking me! I don't care if you're an all-powerful being. You're going to give her back to me."

Dora yelped—although it came out sounding like the roar of a god—as Kieron threw a silver fireball at her. She held up her hands to protect herself out of pure instinct. She waited for the inevitable hit of magic.

After a moment, she peered around her hands when nothing hit her. She widened her eyes. The room was frozen. No one was moving, and the silvery fireball was frozen in the air in front of her, leaving a frozen trail of mist in its wake.

"JESUS!" she muttered.

"Well, he's not quite that, but he is my son."

She looked across at Lucian when she heard him speak. "HOW COME YOU'RE NOT FROZEN TOO?" She walked around the room, peering at the frozen people in it, pausing at Kieron. He looked so upset. She knew she had to fix this. "WILL THEY BE OKAY?"

Lucian nodded. "You just froze time. They won't notice the difference when it resets."

"WHY CAN'T THEY SEE THAT I'M DORA?"

"To them, you look like their idea of god."

"DO I LOOK LIKE A DUDE?" She widened her eyes, quickly glancing down. She was relieved to find that her body looked like hers.

"To most of them, you probably do. Most beings stupidly believe that God has a gender and that it's male."

"HOW DO I STOP BEING GOD?" She sighed. She didn't want this.

"Really, you're quitting already? I thought I was the uncaring slacker." Lucian raised an eyebrow.

"YOU DID THIS TO TEACH ME A LESSON?" she asked incredulously.

He shrugged. "There were a few reasons, but that might have been one."

"YOU'RE AN ASSHOLE! WHAT AM I SUPPOSED TO DO NOW?" She scowled at him.

He shrugged. "That's up to you. You hold the power of the universe in your hands." He nodded at the golden quill in her hand. "What do you want to do?"

"GIVE IT BACK." she muttered.

"Are you certain?"

When she thought about it, she realized that this was the perfect opportunity to fix everything that was wrong with the world. She could save Heaven and Earth. Then she could go home.

"I CAN FIX SOME THINGS FIRST."

He shook his head. "You can try."

She frowned. He didn't seem very optimistic, but she was certain she could do it. Now was the perfect time. With time frozen, she could fix things without worrying about everyone else and then start time again. "HOW DOES IT WORK?"

Lucian shook his head. "There isn't a fucking instruction manual. You just write it and figure it all out yourself." He pointed behind her.

She looked back, noticing the wall of shelves behind the desk. Each shelf was filled with books. She turned and walked over to it, running her fingers along the spines of the books. "WHICH ONE DO I CHOOSE?"

"It doesn't matter. They all index the same place, the infinite universe."

She glanced over her shoulder at him. "THEN WHY HAVE SO MANY BOOKS?"

Looking insulted, he scowled at her. "Because it fucking looks nice."

She rolled her eyes and turned back to the bookshelf. She pulled the nearest book off the shelf and walked over to the desk with it.

When she flipped it open, the pages inside glowed with a golden light. She touched the page with her fingers. It was blank, but she could feel the story inside it. She pressed the tip of the quill to try to write something, and the world she knew fell away.

GOD, THE UNIVERSE AND EVERYTHING

D ora closed her eyes as she was ripped out of the hall. She shot through the sky and out into the universe, coming to an abrupt halt in a dark sky, surrounded by stars as she floated in space.

Lucian, you fucking asshole, what have you done to me?

She turned around, searching for something familiar. There were planets in the distance, and if she focused on them, she could zoom in, heading towards them.

After a few attempts, she realized that she could control where she went with her thoughts.

At super-speed, she zoomed out to the edges of the universe. It wasn't why she was here, but she wanted to see where the universe ended. The further out she zoomed, the more apparent it became that the universe was endless.

After a while, she peered back at where she'd begun, only to discover that her universe was tiny. Earth was just a speck on the shoe of a god. The universe contained so much more than anyone knew.

The knowledge made her feel small. As a human, she was something miniscule on a speck of a planet. No wonder the gods didn't fix things for people. Individuals were so small that they probably didn't see them. It was similar to a human offering protection to an amoeba or a blood cell. No wonder the last God hadn't solved every little problem.

Well this one will do.

Setting her jaw, she zoomed back to Earth. She was going to save all the specks from themselves.

She scanned the different dimensions of her universe. Deciding to fix Heaven first, she zoomed in on Camp Angel, choosing to begin where her problems had started. She headed towards the camp at lightning speed, coming to a halt as she hovered over it staring down at the empty camp below.

All the angels must have flown to God's grotto. She zoomed into the brainwashing facility, passing easily through the walls and locked doors. There were a few blank-eyed angels still bound to gurneys, but it was mostly empty. Those who did remain didn't seem to be able to see her as she floated through the rooms.

With the quill still in her hand, she stopped in one

of the rooms and began to write on the wall:

ALL THE ANGEL'S MINDS WERE RESTORED AS CAMP ANGEL BECAME A BEAUTIFUL GARDEN. WHERE THE ANGELS CAME TO HEAL.

She watched as plants grew in place of sterile walls, flowers blooming around her and lush trees shooting up through the ground. Walking across the green grass, she watched light appear in the eyes of the prisoners as they were released from their restraints, ending up laying on beds of roses.

She smiled. It was perfect.

"Oh, God." One of them moaned as he lay on a giant lily pad on a clear lake that was beside the flowerbeds.

Frowning she walked over to the angel, treading across the water as if it was glass.

"Oh God, save me from these fucking mosquitos." The angel slapped his arm.

Dora scowled at him as he basked under the bright sunshine in paradise, bitching about the fucking mosquitos.

"You're welcome," she muttered as she shook her head.

She turned on her heel and glanced at the wasteland. Containing a shiver, she headed out into the desert, coming to a halt behind one of the zombie scavengers. Now that she was a god, she could see more than just the monster. His cells were all messed up, and his mind was a place of pure torment, half there and half destroyed. He was humming with dark magic, which was trapped inside him. But underneath it all, when you stripped away the decay, he was still a sentient being. He was an angel.

She repaired his cells with a wave of her hand and stripped away the magic. Then she restored his mind.

He cried out as his mind came back, kicking a bloodied carcass away from him in disgust. His wings repaired and turned white, and his eyes shone with holy light.

He fell to his knees and cried, shaking his head.

Dora frowned. He was supposed to be happy, but the memories of what he had done and what had been done to him seemed to be haunting him.

Being careful not to destroy his fragile mind, she removed the memories that would harm him, ensuring that she maintained the ones that made him into the angel he had been before. She weaved through his mind, knotting together his memories in a coherent way, removing the bad ones and keeping the good.

When she was finally done, she smiled when he did. He was back to being the angel he'd been before Camp Angel had gotten hold of him.

She watched him flash his wings before he launched into the sky, this time scavenging for someone he could help.

She rubbed her brow, feeling a headache beginning to form somewhere near her eyebrows. It was tiring fixing all these things, but she knew she had a lot more to fix in this universe.

One down, one hundred to go…

Dora flopped down onto the grass. She knew that the grass wasn't there, not really. But to the physical world, it was, and she felt as if she needed to sit down. Her head hurt. She rubbed her brow. She'd helped hundreds of angels, restoring them to their original forms, removing the restraints on their society.

She'd shut down the corporation. Displaying an impish grin, she recalled the moment when she'd made Fluffers into a flower arranger. He'd oddly seemed happy with his lot in life.

There's nothing that can brighten up my day like seeing a warrior making daisy chains can.

Lettuce was apparently called Trevor, and once his mind had been restored, he turned out to be an incredibly intelligent and gentle soul. For a moment or two, she'd had the feeling that he sensed her there, working away on restoring his mind. Fortunately, he hadn't trusted his own instincts, so she'd remained invisible to him.

After fixing Heaven, removing the burning of the

innocent and all the darkness that had grown here, she was exhausted, and she still had Earth and Hell to fix yet.

Her body wasn't tired. It was her mind. Her mind was exhausted. Fixing some angels, like Lettuce, had been a beautiful experience. But every time she fixed something, someone complained about the change. In fact her proudest moments had been darkened by someone bitching about them. Lucian was right about it being a thankless task. It turned out that it was far easier to point out the flaws in things than it was to create things without flaws. What's more, it was irritating. When you'd worked your ass off to make something better, and some snide asshole—who was doing nothing other than complaining—decided to point out some tiny detail that you'd fucking missed.

It was like curing cancer only to have someone complain that it made them itchy.

Shaking off the disappointment and the exhaustion, she pushed herself up.

Get off your ass, and fix the world.

She passed though the invisible barriers of dimensions, stepping into the Earth she knew. Her arm hurt, and she glanced down at her hand, widening her eyes when she saw golden static sparking between her fingers in an erratic manner.

She shook her arm, trying to shake it off. Pain spiked up her arm, and she cried out as she fell to her knees.

Oh, what the fuck?

As soon as it had appeared, the pain disappeared.

She pushed herself up off the ground, determined to finish this and ignoring the strange tingling through her body.

Come on. Let's get this done.

Narrowing her eyes, she scanned Earth for problems that she could fix, focusing on all of them at once. There were so many bad things happening to so many good people, so much suffering. She started sorting them into categories in her mind, only to find that most of the problems on Earth fell under the categories of greedy and stupid.

As the problems mounted up, her head ached with them all. From the destroyed planet to the capitalist societies, it was a melting pot of destruction and suffering.

No wonder no one else has fixed this mess. Nothing on Earth works properly.

She clenched her jaw, forcing her mind to begin fixing things. Her head began to throb, and her vision blurred.

I probably shouldn't try to fix it all at once, but fuck it. This is going to take a lifetime if I don't.

Ignoring the pain, she forged on.

White pain streaked through her mind, and she fell to her knees screaming. It was too much, too many lives

running through her mind. Too late, she realized that there was too much to do, and she couldn't do it all. The world exploded in a golden light around her as she overloaded.

EXODUS

Dora moaned and rolled over, burying her face in the pillow and trying to ignore the throbbing in her head.

Jesus, what happened to me?

She snuggled into the pillow, smelling the familiar scent of her bed for a moment. Then the memories of being God came flooding back, and she froze.

Inhaling sharply, she rolled over and sat up, now wide-awake.

What the fuck…?

Scanning the room, she widened her eyes. It wasn't her room. It smelled like her pillow, but it wasn't her little pink bed. The bed she lay upon was a stylish double with a black leather headboard and red and white sheets on it.

She cautiously peered over the edge of the bed,

expecting to see a sick pink carpet, but finding polished cherry wood floorboards with a thick white rug on them covering the floor instead.

She ran her fingers over the glass bedside table. The room was beautiful, everything she'd dreamed of. There wasn't a hint of pink or girly tat in it anywhere. It was sleek with a plump leather snuggle chair in the corner near a bookcase. An ornate stone fireplace was beside that on the far wall.

The plain walls were decorated with interesting red and black designs, and the only flowers were a glass vase of real lilies on the windowsill.

Okay, where the fuck am I?

Her pulse raced.

Who's bed am I in?

Quickly scrambling off the bed that she'd been far too comfortable in, she peered down at her clothes, plucking her white camisole off her midriff and peering down at it. This was her nightwear. Gone were the leather pants she'd stolen in Heaven. Now, she wore her red Hello Kitty shorts and matching camisole.

Did someone steal me from my house in my pajamas?

She shook her head. She'd been dead. As far as she knew, she didn't have a body for someone to steal.

She turned to face the bathroom. She couldn't help but admire the stylish dark wood and white tiles as she dashed through the door into the room. It was a nice bathroom. She leaned over the sink and peered at herself in the mirror above the white porcelain sink.

Her hair was a mess of ebony curls, but she looked like herself. She looked human, and more importantly, alive.

Her dark eyes frowned back at her in the mirror. On impulse, she pinched herself.

"Oww," she muttered.

What is this, some kind of Heaven trick?

The last thing she remembered was wanting to fix the world, and then everything had exploded in a golden light.

Her heart thumped in her chest as a bubble of panic swelled in the back of her throat.

What happened to my friends? They were all frozen in time. Where is Kieron?

Running back into the bedroom, she grabbed a pair of jeans off a nearby chair and pulled them on, still fastening them as she rushed out of the room into a stylish corridor.

She slipped on the wooden flooring as she rushed down it, reaching out for the wall for balance.

Seriously, whose fucking house am I in?

She came to an abrupt halt at the top of a spiral staircase, peering over the balustrade at the neat foyer of the designer apartment below.

Unsurely glancing down the corridor and then back over the railing, she wondered where to go first.

But with no idea where she was or why she was here, she tried to be cautious.

It could be the home of a three-eyed monster that eats Goth girls.

Her frown deepened.

Then why was I in its fucking bed?

Shaking her head, she chose to go downstairs. The way out was always downstairs, right? She silently hurried down the spiral staircase, brushing her hand against the wall on her way down.

When she reached the foyer, she eyed the front door. All she had to do was sneak out of it, and she'd be free.

The sound of laughing down the hallway caused her heart to jump into her throat. She froze, trying to decide what she should do. On one hand, she didn't know where she was. She didn't even know what dimension she was in. Was she still in Heaven, Hell or back on Earth?

She set her jaw.

I need to find Kieron. That means I need to find out where this is before I go outside.

Turning towards the sound of laughter, she tiptoed down the hall, heading for it. Her bare feet were silent on the wooden floorboards and thick rugs as she passed a kitchen and a library.

She swallowed as she reached the doorway that the noise was coming out of. She peered around the doorframe, looking inside the room. Like the rest of the apartment, it was stylishly decorated. She discovered a large living room, home to plump leather couches, an ornate fireplace and a widescreen TV.

The laughter was coming from the TV show, which was emanating canned studio laughs at regular intervals.

She could only see the back of the couch. Whoever was sitting on it must be slouched in the seat because she could only see a masculine arm resting on the arm of the couch from this angle.

Either that or the person on the couch is headless.

Swallowing her fear, she gripped a nearby lamp and plucked it off the sideboard, testing the weight of it in her hand.

She rolled her eyes when she had to silently untangle the wire of the lamp and unplug it without being heard.

If this was a horror movie, the monster would appear now while I'm tangled up in fucking lamp cord.

Once the lamp was free of the wall, she took a step towards the couch while quickly wrapping the cord around it.

Maybe I can use it as a whip.

She tried to imagine herself as Indiana Jones and not Kieron's grandmother with a whip as she continued walking towards the couch, dreading what she would find there. She knew she had to face whatever she found here. Speaking to whatever lived here was the only way she could find out where she was, what happened to Pooey, and it was the only way she could find Kieron.

Galvanized by the last thought, she stepped beside the patron of the couch. She turned to face them with the lamp raised, ready to fight for her friends. They'd saved her over and over again. This time she was going to save them from whatever fucked up reality the universe had served them.

Her eyes widened as she peered down at a sleeping Kieron, slumped on the couch. His arms were wrapped around a large cushion as he cuddled it. His lips were turned up with a hint of a smile as he slept peacefully, a light snore coming from him at regular intervals.

She lowered the lamp and placed it on a nearby coffee table, her eyes never leaving his bare-chested form. She wasn't sure how he managed to look adorable and sexy at the same time, but that was just Kieron. His blue jeans hung low on his hips, and the muscles in his chest occasionally twitched.

While contemplating waking him up, she noticed his eyelids flutter. She patiently waited for his eyes to open. His dark lashes fluttered over cerulean blue eyes before slowly opening. He smiled dreamily at her, half-asleep and half-awake.

Then his eyes widened, and he shot awake, abruptly sitting up and staring around. "You exploded!"

"What?" she asked, alarmed by the revelation. To be fair, her last moments as God had felt as if she'd exploded, but Kieron hadn't been there. How could he have known that?

"You picked up that pen, exploded, and some old dude took your place." He scanned her before jumping to his feet and gripping her arms. He ran his hands up and down them as if to check they were real before he hauled her against him into a tight embrace.

"No, wait. I was the old guy," she mumbled into his chest.

He froze. Then he released her and stepped back, eyeing her with concern. "Wut?"

"I became God." She tried to explain.

"You became a dude?" He widened his eyes.

"Well, no. You just saw a dude because that's what you think God looks like."

"So you became a dude." He frowned.

"No, I did not become a fucking dude!" She shook her head. "It was just an illusion."

"You looked like a dude." He shrugged.

"I've got a better question." Pooey's voice echoed from the doorway. "What the fuck do I look like to you?"

ora spun around to see a little red-haired person scowling in the doorway. She widened her eyes. "Pooey?"

He narrowed his eyes even more. "Who the fuck else could I be? What the hell am I?" His little fingers clenched into a fist as a vein throbbed in his temple.

Dora scanned him. He was a cute person of small stature. "You're a little person."

"You look like a dwarf," Kieron said.

She groaned. "No, the correct term is little person."

Pooey's eyes widened. "What, like one of those short, fat things in World of Warcraft?"

"You're not fat," Dora quickly said. He wasn't. He looked great, even if he was a bit on the short side.

"So this is God's punishment for me." Pooey nodded. "He made me into a short, fat, ginger twat. Fuckin' wanker!"

"Dora was God and a dude." Kieron turned to face her. "Why did you make Pooey into a short, fat, ginger twat?" he asked, displaying an earnest expression.

"I didn't, and I wasn't a dude!" She shook her head. "I don't know what has happened. I was God. I fixed Heaven, and then I er, overloaded or something. Next thing, I woke up here."

"And made me into a ginger twat?" Pooey asked.

"No! Be thankful that neither of you are still frozen."

"You froze us?" Kieron asked with wide eyes.

"No, I froze time, but er, you were in it. So the last time I saw you, you were kinda frozen in Heaven." She winced.

"So where are we now?" Pooey asked.

Dora frowned, looking around the room. Her eyes settled on the widescreen TV as the news appeared on it. It didn't take her long to realize this was Earth. She recognized the channel. "We're on Earth by the looks of it."

"Wait, so are we human now?" Kieron frowned.

Dora felt her spirits lift. Was she human, had she finally come home as a human being?

"Oh hell, no!" Kieron cried.

She turned to see Kieron scrunching up his face in

concentration.

"What are you doing?"

"My horns, I can't summon them!" He patted his head. "Are they there? Can you see any of them?"

"Your wings are gone too," Pooey said, pointing to his back.

"Fuck them. Dora, help me find my horns. I can't live as a human, I just can't!" Kieron stared at her with a helpless look in his big blue eyes.

She patted his golden hair. There were no horns in them. "Maybe they're just not active or something. You'll be okay."

"B-but I'll just be a human." He widened his eyes. "I don't even know what humans do!"

"They live." She shrugged. "It's not so bad."

He narrowed his eyes. "Don't they die too?"

"Yeah, but then they go to Hell," she said.

He sighed. "It's not an ideal situation."

"You can have some fun before you have to learn to be evil. Trust me. Old people do evil better than anyone else. After a lifetime of disappointment, you really get a handle on being mean. It might help you learn evil."

"How does it work?" he asked, curiosity lighting up his eyes.

"Well, you have fun and try your best. That's how it starts. Then I think you fuck up a lot. That's really easy to do as a human. Then when you're completely

243

screwed, the disappointment kicks in, and you get bitter. Evil kind of comes naturally to you at that point." She frowned, wondering if this was the worst advice she had ever given anyone.

"She's right," Pooey said. "That's how I mastered evil."

Kieron nodded. "Fine, I'll stay human for now, but the second I don't like it, I'm getting my horns back."

Dora tried to summon Kieron's demon powers since he appeared to be so miserable without them, but nothing happened. Anything godly had left her. Judging by the story on the news about fracking, she hadn't saved the world from all the bad shit in it either.

She idly wondered who was God now. Was anyone God, or had she burned up the quill with overuse?

"I guess we're all just human now," she muttered.

Pooey raised his hand. He stared intently at it for a moment before conjuring a ball of golden light in the palm of his hand. "Maybe not, my bitches."

Kieron widened his eyes. "You have golden powers! Are you God now?"

Pooey shrugged. "Fucked if I know."

"Restore my horns," Kieron demanded.

Pooey glanced at Dora, and she nodded. Kieron wouldn't be happy as a human.

Shrugging, Pooey shot a blast of golden light at Kieron.

He smiled and stretched, his eyes glowed red for a moment, and then his tiny horns popped out of the top of his head. Unfortunately, a pair of giant white wings shot out of his back at the same time. "That feels better." He smiled, clearly unaware that he was still half angel.

Pooey winced.

Dora nodded. "Yeah, you look more like your old self." She didn't have the heart to tell him that he was still an angel too.

"What about you?" Pooey asked her.

She shook her head. "I'm happy as a human."

He shrugged, and then cast a golden light on himself. "Did it work?"

"You still look like a short, fat, ginger twat." Kieron said.

Pooey scowled, shook his hand as if trying to jolt the batteries, and then tried again.

Dora shook her head. Whatever magical powers Pooey had, they weren't Godly powers. He couldn't change his own form with them.

"This is some fucking bullshit!" Pooey said as he dropped his arm and hung his head in defeat.

"What do we do now?" Kieron asked.

"We need to figure out where we are." Dora picked up the nearby phone.

"How are we going to do that?" Pooey asked.

"I'm gonna ask my dad." She dialed the phone

number for her father's church, hoping he was still in it.

"Hey, dad," she said when he picked up.

"Dora?" he asked.

"Yeah, it's Dora—"

"Your mother wants to know when you're picking up your laundry."

"What laundry?" She frowned. He didn't sound surprised to hear from her, especially considering that the last time he'd seen her, she'd died.

"I know you and your friends are sharing a house during college, but you can't use your mother as a free laundry service." Her father admonished. "If you're old enough for your own apartment, then you're old enough to do your own laundry."

"Right, I'm at college now." Dora frowned at Kieron. Time appeared to have passed without them being in it. The world was different by the sound of it. "So er, dad, what's my address now?"

"What?"

"I mean, where are you forwarding my mail to? I just want to check you have the right address..." She shrugged.

If in doubt, bullshit your way out.

"It's that new complex near the college. Your little ginger friend who owns the apartment gave me the address. It's here somewhere. Um yep, here's the address: 66B Hellsgate Apartments, Sixth Street. Does that sound right?"

Dora nodded. "Yeah, that sounds right, Dad. Thanks." A slow smile spread on her face. She had her own place. She had a red room. She lived with her best friends. It was everything she'd ever dreamed of.

She said goodbye to her dad and then hung up before turning around and beaming a smile at Kieron and Pooey. "This is our apartment! We live here, together."

Kieron grinned. "We moved in together then." He slipped an arm around her waist.

Pooey headed over to the couch before jumping on it and sitting down. "I get to live with you two, fuckin' awesome. Go get me some cheesy puffs."

Kieron and Dora sat beside him. They all stared blankly at the TV for a moment.

"So, is that it?" Dora asked. "Is that all the crazy Heaven and Hell shit over with now?"

"Probably not, I've still got magic," Pooey said.

"I'm still a demon," Kieron said.

"I'm still a fail-witch." Dora laughed. Then she sank back against Kieron. She was happy. For the first time in her life, she was content. Sure, there was crazy shit around every corner, and she was certain there would be more to come. But right now, she was alive, safe and with her best friends. Life was great. She was happy to be alive. She was happy to be home. She was happy that she wasn't a god. She sank into the couch.

For the first time in her life, she was in the right place at the right time and with the right people. This was where she belonged. This was her home.

Kieron hugged her against him, and then he kissed her on the top of her head.

"You know what I don't get," Pooey said.

They both glanced over at him.

"What the fuck happened to Lucian?"

THE FALLEN ONE

Lucian screamed as he dropped out of Heaven, falling at high-speed towards Earth.

"Fuuuuck!" He tried to summon any kind of power to save himself, but since that stupid fucking girl had locked up his powers, he'd been powerless to change anything.

Sure, she might have fixed Heaven, but she royally screwed up the universe when she overloaded. She'd passed on his powers to the older gods, and they'd cast his ass out of Heaven.

"I made this fucking place! You can't throw me out of it!" He shouted at a cloud as he passed it by.

The face of an older god materialized in the fluffy cloud. It simply smiled at him.

"Oh, fuck you!" he cried. Then he glanced down and yelped.

Below him, the ocean drew closer and closer.

"You don't even understand gravity. Give me my fucking powers, or I'll come into Heaven anyway, idiot!"

A bolt of lightning slammed into his back, and he cried out as the power surged through him.

Awesome, they're going to fucking electrocute me.

His pulse raced as he plopped into the ocean with a loud splat, the impact causing his teeth to rattle.

He panicked for a moment as he sank. But when he stopped struggling, he realized that he didn't need to breathe. It took him a few moments to figure it out, but he eventually realized that they had given him back some of his powers when they shot him in the back.

Breathing a sigh, he swam up to the surface. He bobbed for a while, trying to determine the best direction to head in. When he saw land ahead of him, he swam towards it.

Exhausted by the time he reached a nearby beach, he dragged himself through the surf before flopping onto the beach with the sun burning down on his back.

He tried to summon his powers, struggling to muster the energy to summon anything. After a moment, he gave up. Whatever power he had was diluted now. He sank into the sand in defeat.

This is going to suck.

THE END

READ KIERON'S STORY

A CHRISTMAS STORY IN THE DEMON DIARIES

A HINT of

HELL

BEWITCHED BY CHRISTMAS

CLAIRE CHILTON

He's just failed at being evil...

Kieron Lascher thought his life as a minor demon lord in Hell couldn't get any worse, but when he fails his exams and is sent into another realm as punishment by his parents, he realizes there are worse places than Hell.

With deadly beasts and evil Satan Claws roaming the frosty land, Kieron has to fight to survive. With the help of a banished succubus, he learns that he needs to find the missing codex to gain some power.

If he manages to take out Satan Claws and learn pure evil, he might be able to open a portal and go back home. But first, he has to master being truly evil to some cute little elves. That won't be difficult for a demon lord, right?

WWW.CLAIRE-CHILTON.COM

CAN'T WAIT FOR CLAIRE CHILTON'S NEXT STORY?

Let her know by leaving stars and telling her what
you liked about

DIVINE DORA

in a review!

FREE BOOKS

Enjoy Claire Chilton's free books. Try out her
other series for free or read more of this series on
any device with **Free Reads**.

claire-chilton.com/free-books

WANT TO TALK TO OTHER FANS?

Visit *claire-chilton.com* and join the discussion.

AUTHOR

After completing her honors degree in English Literature, Claire Chilton was interviewed to work for MI5. Fortunately, for the sake of the United Kingdom, she did not get the job. Now a web designer and graphic designer with a passion for great stories, she writes about the adventures she'd like to have.

A prolific writer with wide-ranging interests, Claire specializes in romantic and speculative fiction, which includes genres such as mystery, science fiction, fantasy, horror, comedy and romance. Her mystery romance novel, *Hustle*, won Harlequin's *So You Think You Can Write* contest in 2013, and her previous books in *The Demon Diaries* won the *Most Read* award on Wattpad.

After exploring the world in her misspent youth, traveling across Europe, Africa, and the Caribbean, she now lives in an ancient Roman city in Yorkshire with her Californian husband and a fluffy kitten called Shadow, who is convinced she is a bigger cat than she is.

You can find Claire online at **claire-chilton.com**.